"I miss you, Cleo," Romaine said. "And I can't make myself stop loving you. Can't we try just one more time, please?"

Cleo looked at her, feeling sadness rise up. *If only I could trust you. If only I could make myself forget all the times you've hurt me.* "You have driven me to the brink of madness and back. You've hurt me more times than I care to remember, and still I love you, will always love you. But this time is different."

"Different? Different because you're in love with someone else?"

"Yes. How many times did you think you could run away and expect me to wait? Romaine, I'm done waiting."

"What if I'm not done loving you? What if I can't make myself stop loving you? Cleo, I want you back," Romaine said, moving closer.

"I'm not coming back."

"You can say that, but I know better," Romaine said, pressing her up against the counter. She nestled between thighs she now longed for. She started to unbutton Cleo's shirt.

"Dammit, Romaine, I'm not one of your playthings. Don't treat me like one," Cleo said, trying to get away. Romaine held her tight.

"You want me. I know you do. Don't play coy with me. I know you miss me," Romaine said, kissing her and continuing her pursuit.

The doorbell rang.

"Let me go!"

OLD TIES

SAXON BENNETT

THE NAIAD PRESS, INC.
1997

Copyright © 1997 by Saxon Bennett

All rights reserved. No part of this book may be reproduced or transmitted in any form or by any means, electronic or mechanical, including photocopying, without permission in writing from the publisher.

Printed in the United States of America on acid-free paper
First Edition

Editor: Lisa Epson
Cover designer: Bonnie Liss (Phoenix Graphics)
Typesetter: Sandi Stancil

Library of Congress Cataloging-in-Publication Data

Bennett, Saxon, 1961 –
   Old ties / Saxon Bennett.
     p.   cm.
   ISBN 1-56280-159-7
   1. Lesbians—Fiction. I. Title.
PS3552.E54754404   1997
813'.54—dc21   96-39471
                                                          CIP

To Brenda for knowing when to say when and for remembering what was good.

To the best partner a gal can have, Lin, thanks for your patience, faith and love.

To my furry friend Sir J.H. Crappapore for those precious moments when we write together, what would I do without your long slinky tail in my face.

ABOUT THE AUTHOR

My mother didn't like my last explanation of self. She said there was more to me than reading, writing, riding, gardening, and fucking, not necessarily in that order. And she's right. I thought long and hard and decided that I don't write personal ads very well. More to me? I looked around corners and behind doors, thought of myself when I was a thirteen-year-old tyrant, or a sweet baby-faced child, already at war with the world, the anomaly I am today. More to me? I don't know, gentle reader: if you find those parts please send them back as I don't have a spare.

One

Cleo Wetherfield sat at the counter of Cactus Jack's Restaurant and waited for her coffee. She owned the restaurant, or rather half of it. Romaine owned the other half, which was fine when they were together, or when they were getting along. Now was not one of those times.

It was the waitress's first day. Cleo hired her because her name was Frankie. She liked people with strange names because she hated her own. She always imagined her mother heavy with child desperately in search of a name. Cleo was convinced her mother found her name in one of those sixty-nine-cent name books found at the checkout counter.

Cleo was a name carelessly chosen from a paperback, lacking the grace of ancestry, and she was stuck with it until the worms picnicked on her eyeballs. Even then the name would be on the tombstone. Maybe she should put "Here lies the badly named" and let people wonder.

Frankie was named after Franklin D. Roosevelt. People always smiled at that and asked her if her mother had wanted a boy, but she hadn't. She fully intended on having a girl. She wanted a girl with spunk. "A girl named after a famous man full of good traits would be filled to the brim with spunk." The choice still didn't make sense, but Frankie's mother was not a woman of sense. She was a woman with guts. If the gut wanted it the mind followed, cowed by the sheer force of innate desire.

Cleo also hired her because Frankie was musically inclined. When Frankie wrote "singer" in the section marked "special talents" on the application, Cleo was sold. The restaurant had a Friday-night talent show. You didn't have to be good. You had to try. Trying counted. The talent show boasted poets, writers, performance artists, and comedians; some of them were even funny.

But the real reason Frankie got the job was because she was cute. She was younger than Cleo, but then Cleo was pushing forty-something. Frankie had dark, shoulder-length hair combed into a ponytail and blue eyes.

Cleo loved blue eyes. Romaine had blue eyes too. Twenty years ago, Cleo had fallen in love with those eyes and had yet to retrieve herself from their captivating gaze. Cleo's eyes were dark. *We always want what we don't have.* Cleo knew hiring a cute, talented waitress was going to piss Romaine off, which was precisely why she did it.

Frankie finally figured out the coffee maker and returned with Cleo's coffee.

"Thank you. So how do you like the job so far?" Cleo asked, trying to be sociable though her heart wasn't in it. *Funny,* she thought, the older one gets, the more stock phrases one disguises as social graces.

"It's fine. I haven't been through a lunch rush yet, so I guess we'll see."

"It's the evening cocktail hour I'd worry about. Living here makes most of us highly dependent on diversions. Choose your poison."

"A town with a drinking problem?"

"Let's just say we have the European sensibility of taking the nip off the day and, in this case, every day."

"I see."

"How in god's name did you end up here anyway?"

"My aunt lives here."

"Let me guess, you left a bad relationship, female perhaps, and now you want to spend the summer forgetting. Am I close?"

"Right on target. Is it that obvious?"

"No, but that's how most of us end up here. We leave the city hoping for some peace and quiet and the chance to forget."

"How long have you been here?"

"Too long. Oh shit!"

"What?"

"It's Romaine."

"Is she your girlfriend?"

"Ex-wife, twice removed."

Romaine Little strode into the restaurant quickly, her boots striking the hardwood floor with even precision.

"I want an explanation, and I want it now."

"Have some coffee," Cleo offered, looking at Frankie.

"I don't want any fucking coffee. I want answers. I want to know why you sent a box full of my panties cut into very small pieces to my studio. My receptionist opened it with the morning mail."

"Maybe you shouldn't let your receptionist open your mail."

"Why did you do that?"

"Because I'm mad. I told you to get your shit out of my house. But you were in such a hurry to hop into bed with your latest fling that you couldn't be bothered. I figured you were obviously having such a good time with your pants off that you couldn't be bothered with panties. I thought I was doing you a favor."

Romaine grabbed her wrist as Cleo picked up her coffee cup.

"Don't start, Romaine. I'm not yours to do that to anymore. Remember?"

Romaine squeezed hard, clenched her jaw, and let go, sending coffee oozing across the counter.

"I'll come get my stuff."

"Don't bother. I had it sent to the studio."

Romaine glared at her and marched to the door. She turned. "Times like these, I don't wonder why we can't make it work."

"Romaine, go fuck yourself!" Cleo said without turning around.

Frankie simply looked at Cleo.

"Will you please hand me a towel?"

"Are you all right?" Frankie asked, mopping up the coffee.

"I'm fine. But I would like some more coffee."

Alice strolled in. In her late forties, she was slim with dark hair graying slightly at the temples. She dressed like a bad drag queen. Her butch girlfriends thought she was the femme to die for. Cleo didn't understand it, but then go figure with lesbians. There's no accounting for taste. Cleo had gone out with Romaine. Figure that one.

"Quite the outfit," Cleo murmured under her breath.

"I heard that. At least I don't wander around in men's underclothing," Alice replied, snarling.

It was true. Cleo wore only boxers and men's undershirts, with a tie if the occasion was festive. Frankie wondered about the ensemble but was too polite to ask.

"I only do it to piss Romaine off. She hates it, which of course forces me to do it. Besides, I've quite a collection. It's a hard habit to leave off."

"Was that Romaine I saw flying out of here on her little black broom?" Alice asked.

"You're so astute. She's mad at me 'cause I ripped up all her expensive little undies and sent them to her at work. Bad girl. But I couldn't resist. Call me silly."

"My god, you are the worst."

"That's why you love me so," Cleo said, smiling and scrunching up her shoulders.

Alice looked at her. "Haven't you some gardening to do?"

"It's a good thing you're the manager or the place would have gone under years ago. I've no sense of time management, and all Romaine wants to do is fuck every little strumpet that strolls into town."

"Remember that next time I'm up for a raise," Alice said, shooing her out the door.

"Good luck with the lunch rush, Frankie," Cleo called out as Alice shoved her out the back door. "She sure is cute, don't you think, Alice?"

"She's not my type. I like men, not little boys."

"I have a penchant for the less-than-lipstick, not-been-'round-the-block-more-than-once woman-child."

"And how do you know she is one?"

"She has that air of innocence about her, and she only wears Chap Stick. I checked."

"So what do you think of our owners? Crazy bunch, but they're harmless," Alice said, leaning on the counter.

"Romaine didn't look harmless."

"Oh that. Well yeah, they've had a few knock-down-drag-outs. But the police have only locked them up once. Most of the time it's a bit of broken crockery or a window, flattened car tires, and let's see... One time Romaine threw every bit of glassware and crockery in the entire restaurant at Cleo. It was starting to look kind of cheesy anyway and needed to be replaced."

"How long have they been at this?"

"The last twenty years. On for seven, off for

three, on for another seven, then off for two, then on for a year, is that twenty? I think I've got it right."

"Are they still trying work out the fine details?"

"I don't understand it myself. They were each other's first lover, and they can't seem to let it go. Romaine goes out with other people; Cleo waits around until she's done; and they start all over again. Sick, huh?"

"Different. How come Cleo doesn't go out with anyone?"

"She calls herself a serial monogamist or some such nonsense. She thinks she mated for life, and so she waits."

"That's not healthy," Frankie said, cleaning up the counter. "What should I do next?"

"Are you much of a prep cook? Seems we're a little short today. I hate chopping veggies. Do you mind?"

"No, not at all."

"Cleo should have a load of stuff for you to chop."

"I've never worked in a restaurant before. Cleo told you that, didn't she?"

"Oh, yeah. It doesn't matter. Folks 'round here aren't picky. Cleo hired you because you're cute, not because you're qualified."

"Oh," Frankie said, making her way back to the kitchen.

Two

Cleo sat on the front porch in her favorite chair, rocking back and forth furiously.

"Why do I let her do this to me?" Cleo said aloud. "I must be stupid, insane, out of control. I just wish I could understand why I don't get up and walk away when she dumps me. Why doesn't the hurt get less with each one? You'd think I'd be long past caring. Why do I let her march back into my life when she's finished with her playmates?"

Cleo asked herself these questions each time it happened, and to each question she knew the answer.

"I wait because I love her. I hurt because I love her. I let her come back because I love her."

Sometimes when Romaine went away it was a relief. Cleo would hurt, and then she would begin to enjoy the pain, almost relishing the loneliness. Any good therapist would say her behavior was sick and wrong but that it had a productive side because she got to know herself best during these masochistic periods. When she began to rebuild her life, Romaine would stroll home and beg forgiveness. And the whole vicious cycle would begin again.

It was like having a new lover with the familiarity of an old one. Romaine would return with new experiences to share, and Cleo would fall in love with her all over again. Cleo avoided the fear of new relationships because Romaine was her oldest and best friend, her only lover. Loving Romaine was Cleo's major fault.

Cleo was a coward. New things made her nervous, so she surrounded herself with old, comfortable things, and Romaine was one of these, her little lettuce head. She was Puddle and Romaine was Lettuce. How could she have another lover?

Who would call her Puddle? Who would she cry out for in the night, half-witted from one of her nightmares, if Lettuce wasn't there? What if she awoke to some other woman, a veritable stranger, in her bed? She knew she couldn't do it. She would wait again and again for Romaine to return.

Her rocking slowed as she remembered the falling-in-love times. Romaine was wonderful when she was in love. She was decent then, taking her incredible wrath out on others, saving her sweet part for you.

Romaine had an angry streak that ran deep,

traceable to something about a witch of a mother. It was hard to tell where Romaine's anger came from because she had disowned her family when she was twenty. Cleo had never met them. Romaine had Cleo and her old girlfriends for family, and that was all the family she needed.

The other sick part of the arrangement was that the girlfriends all knew one another and in most cases were friends, living in town or close by. A bunch of incestuous lesbians, sleeping with each other, trading partners, all having made love to the same woman. Cleo was the only untainted one of the bunch, not that some of them hadn't tried. Bobbi had tried for three years.

When Romaine started staying out late and then being nasty to Bobbi when she did get home, Bobbi had gone to see Cleo, to talk, cry, and have a hand to hold. Cleo was there to pick up the pieces when Romaine broke it off, and Cleo and Bobbi became friends. Cleo liked Bobbi, liked her a lot. Bobbi wanted to be lovers, and she hounded Cleo.

Bobbi thought they were dating. They went to the bar together, to dinner, to the movies. They even went on weekend getaways, but to no avail. Cleo wouldn't sleep with Bobbi. Sometimes when they were out picnicking, they would lie on their backs, stare up at the clouds, and play the cloud game. Cleo held Bobbi's hand and was quite happy, but that was all she wanted. She wanted a friend to love, not a lover to fuck.

Sex always seemed to muck things up. With friends you could be yourself; being lovers meant you had to hide things. Cleo loved Bobbi too much to do that.

One night she almost succumbed. She made Bobbi dinner at her house, her beautiful house, the empty farmhouse no one wanted, the one she had built up from almost nothing. It had been sitting empty the day she drove past in her bright yellow truck. Broken windows were gaping holes, black and empty. Cleo felt an instant affinity. She had to have that house. It took years to get the house the way she wanted. But it was truly a labor of love. She made it beautiful, made it glisten and shine with care and pride. Cleo had precious few visitors because only special people got an invite. Bobbi was special.

They made dinner and afterward they lay on the living room rug finishing off the blackberry wine Cleo had made.

"Why won't you let me seduce you?"

"Because it would spoil a perfectly good friendship."

"No, it wouldn't. I love you. I want you. We could still be friends."

"Until we broke up and you wouldn't speak to me. I guarantee you, this is better."

"No, this is platonic, prepubescent lust with no end in sight. This is frustration and futility."

"See, when you talk about sex you change."

"I know. I'm sorry. But I still wish you'd let me seduce you."

What Bobbi didn't know and what would keep Cleo safe was that discussing the probabilities of sex ruined it for Cleo. If Bobbi had been more like

Romaine, she would have scooped Cleo up in her loving arms and carried her off to bed, saying nothing and kissing defenses from her lover's lips.

After another bottle of blackberry wine that almost happened.

Bobbi poured Cleo another glass of wine, waited for her to finish, and then kissed her. Bobbi didn't stop until she felt Cleo kiss her back. Bobbi felt the darting precision of Cleo's tongue and waited for the soft moans she knew would come. She kissed Cleo's ears, her neck, her breasts, those lovely breasts she longed for daily. She loosed them from their hiding place and kissed them. She kissed Cleo's flat, hard stomach with its carefully sculpted navel that whispered welcome. Cleo sat up.

"No, no, I can't," Cleo said, starting to cry. Her dark eyes filled with sadness. Bobbi held her and never touched her again.

They joked about it later, how Bobbi and she made torso love and that it had been nice.

That evening was the closest infidelity Cleo ever committed against Romaine. Even though Romaine was sleeping with Sheila then, when Romaine found out, she cornered Cleo in her studio.

"So what's this about you and Bobbi? Are you dating or, better yet, sleeping together?"

"No, we're just friends. Contrary to you, I love my friends, but I don't make love to them. There's only one woman for me, and she won't have me."

Romaine sat on the corner of her desk and reached out for Cleo, who walked willingly into her arms, nestling her face in Romaine's dark hair.

"I miss you," Romaine whispered. "And I still love you."

Romaine carried her off to bed, finishing what Bobbi had started.

Cleo watched the sun set behind the red rock cliffs, their vibrant color growing muted as the light faded. It was the first time they made love while Romaine lived with another woman, but it was not the last. She remembered lying in Romaine's arms wondering what it meant. Was it infidelity? Romaine had girlfriends, but Cleo was her wife. Sometimes they didn't live together, but they never stopped loving each other.

She remembered the shadows of clouds from the skylight windows passing across their naked bodies. She remembered being satiated yet wanting more. She had rolled on top of Romaine and ardently seduced her again and again, until they both lay panting, glistening with the sheen of desire. It was as if Cleo was drowning, and making Romaine come was her only lifeline.

Sheila couldn't hope to compare. Romaine kept wandering back to Cleo's bed to get another taste of that sweet, sweet stuff.

Perhaps that was why Bobbi wanted Cleo. Perhaps that was why Sheila never looked directly at Cleo. Cleo possessed something that they did not, and they craved it.

When Romaine missed Cleo, she missed her loving. She missed the way Cleo made her feel. There was something about her that Romaine couldn't get out of her system. Maybe the girlfriends were an attempt to exorcise herself. It had yet to work, though through the years Romaine had tried diligently.

Whenever Romaine told her this, Cleo looked away. She had nothing to compare herself with. When she made love to Romaine she reached deep down inside her. She touched her light, held it in her hands, stroked its softness, cooed her love. Romaine would cry out, hold her tight, and beg for more, soaring into the universe.

Cleo stopped rocking and dropped her head in her hands. That was how Frankie found her, lost, wandering aimlessly through her memories, knowing she was as much Romaine's invention as she was her own. How could she possibly separate the two?

"I didn't know you lived here," Frankie called from across the gate.

"Now you do. Where do you live?"

"Two blocks down on Howard."

"What are you doing?"

"Going home."

"Then what are you going to do?"

"Have a beer," Frankie said, stuffing her hands in her pockets.

"Why don't you have one with me? You know I'm harmless. I'm sure Alice has told you the story. And she wonders why I don't get dates."

"I thought you didn't want them."

"I don't. I wouldn't know what to do anyway."

Frankie opened the little green gate and walked up to the porch. "I guess I could have a beer so long as you're harmless."

Cleo brought her a beer.

"Is it true that you and Romaine have been lovers off and on for twenty years?"

"Unfortunately it is, and unfortunately many people have gotten hurt in the process. It's an endless perverted game we play. See that you don't get yourself caught up in it. Romaine always takes a shine to the new girl in town."

"Are you telling me this so I won't go out with your wife or because you don't want me to get hurt in the cross fire?"

"I don't want you to get hurt."

"Why?"

"Because I think I might like you, given the chance."

Three

On Friday night the singing waitress was out front waiting for the show to start.

"Are you nervous?" Cleo asked.

"I'm always nervous," Frankie said, clearing her throat.

Alice announced her and Frankie went in, giving Cleo one last look.

Cleo smiled at her. "You'll do fine."

"I hope you're right."

* * * * *

Cleo sat at the bar. She ordered a shot of tequila with a beer chaser. Romaine, with her new girlie, would inevitably be there. Cleo wanted to be firmly anesthetized, not that Cynthia really mattered. She was a fill-in and a payback.

Romaine was angry with Cleo over issues of trust. After their last breakup, Cleo had refused to surrender certain freedoms and certain pieces of property, namely, the house. She told Romaine she was tired of dividing things up. She wanted them to keep things separate. It would be easier. The breaking point had been the house.

Romaine wanted her to sell it so they could buy property out of town and build another house. Cleo refused. The house meant everything to her. Seven years of sorrow went into rebuilding it and making it her own. It was as if Romaine was asking her to sell her very skin. Romaine accused her of loving the house more than she loved her. Cleo did. *I can count on waking up to my house, I can't say the same thing about you,* she thought. Romaine couldn't understand why Cleo didn't trust her.

Everyone else did. Romaine had spent the last twenty years falling in and out of love with Cleo and then breaking her heart each time. "Honey, hang on to the house," Alice told her. Bobbi, who hated Romaine with more fervor than Cleo ever mustered, thought Cleo crazy for going back.

Romaine had a memory quickly selective to forget the pain she put her lovers through. She expected absolution and was angry when most weren't willing to give it. Cleo was the only one stupid enough to forgive the transgressions. But Romaine didn't know that each time she broke Cleo's heart, there was less of it left to give the next time. Cleo loved Romaine and she would always love her, but each time she kept more pieces of herself hidden so there would be less to hurt when Romaine walked.

All the lezzies, as the local straight population referred to them, thought Cleo the strangest creature for putting up with it. Half of them had gone out with Romaine, but Cleo's little eccentricities and generous nature won them over. They soon forgot who she went home with.

Frankie started to sing. She looked good up there, her loose dark hair hiding one side of her face and her leather jacket sloping off one shoulder as she played. She sat on a stool, one sandal kicked off, her toes wrapped around the stay. Cleo was admiring the song with its simple lyrics and sparse acoustics when Romaine and Cynthia strolled in arm in arm.

Cleo sat listening, trying to ignore them. The first time out was always the hardest. She had experience on her side now. The first time Romaine had left and Cleo had seen another woman on her arm, it had nearly killed her. Cleo had drunk herself blind, gone outside, and thrown up.

She remembered looking at her vomit-covered shoes through teary eyes. That was what being in love did to you. She vowed never to fall for another woman. It didn't count that she kept taking Romaine back; that was the same old, tired love. It wasn't new love. As long as she stayed away from new love, she'd be okay. She'd been successful thus far.

Romaine was in a mood for paybacks. She kept

touching and kissing Cynthia, making sure Cleo would see. Cleo rolled her eyes and took her beer outside, saving Romaine the public humiliation of mauling her girlfriend. Alice watched her go; so did Frankie. Frankie turned back to her guitar. When she looked up again, Cleo was standing outside the open window watching her. They made eye contact, and Cleo smiled.

After the show Frankie went out to see if Cleo was still around. She found her, feet up, Birkenstocks kicked off, drinking a beer on one of the couches on the veranda of the old-house-turned-restaurant.

"Good show."

"You liked it?"

"Of course. It was sensitive without being sappy; it was ironic and sarcastic without being abusive. I like that. You'll be a great star someday, I'm certain."

"Yeah, sure," Frankie said, sitting down.

"Don't sell yourself short."

"Why not? You do it all the time. Why do you put up with her?"

"Romaine?"

"Yeah, it's not like she has to flaunt her girlfriend or anything."

"Oh that. It's a payback for the undies. It's no big deal. Can I buy you a beer?"

"Sure."

They sat talking and drinking until it got late. Romaine and Cynthia came out the door and looked over at them.

"Romaine, Cynthia," Cleo said.

"Hello, Cleo, and I'm sorry I didn't catch your name?" Romaine said, giving Frankie a cold stare.

"Her name is Frankie. You'll remember that when she's famous for her delicate lyrics," Cleo said, gently slapping her leg.

"I'm sure. Good night, ladies," Romaine snarled.

"Isn't she a treat?" Cleo said good-naturedly. "Are you hungry?"

"Sure," Frankie said.

"Let's go to the five and diner and get some breakfast. You don't have plans do you?"

"In this town, are you high?"

"No, but I wouldn't mind. Maybe we'll do that later."

Frankie sat across the table from Cleo, sipping coffee and waiting for their breakfast.

"Now that you know all about me, I think it's time you shared something. If that's all right with you."

"It's no big secret. Breakup after three years, tried seeing other people, got sick of my job, and I needed a break."

"Slim pickings, dear. She doesn't have a name? You don't know what went wrong?"

"She was bored. Her name was Electra. That wasn't her real name, of course. She was an actress in off, off, and more off plays around San Francisco."

"You mean to tell me you left the lesbian mecca of the West Coast to come to a small town in southern Utah. You must be completely mad."

"It's beautiful here, and I needed a break. Why do you stay here?"

"Because city life makes me tense and uptight, and the smog hurts my sinuses. Besides, all I really want to do is garden, take care of my house, read, and hike about on the Red Cliffs. A perfect little recluse. I can't do those things in the city. I do travel, I want you to know. I'm not your average run-of-the-mill hick. I'm a citified hick, more like certified. You'll have to come see my map sometime of all the places I've been."

The waitress brought over their food.

"I hear she's done it again," Theresa, the waitress, said.

"That's the only bad thing about small-town life. Everyone knows everything," Cleo said, switching her plate with Frankie's. Theresa never got the orders right. Actually you were lucky if you got what you ordered at your table and not the next one over.

"It's a reporter this time?"

"I believe so. I haven't perused her résumé, but it's something like that. Theresa, meet my new friend Frankie," Cleo said, hoping her inquisitive friend would get the hint.

Theresa smiled at Frankie.

"You don't want to talk about it?"

"You got it."

"You two should really give it up," Theresa said, shaking her head as if she were talking counsel from forces greater than herself.

"Now there's a novel idea," Cleo muttered.

Fortunately, Earl Holland screamed from across the room.

"Do you think I could get some coffee 'round here?" he bellowed.

"Doesn't it bother you that your love life is the subject of so much discussion?" Frankie asked.

"It's not my favorite thing. But what am I going to do? Anyway, I thought we were going to talk about you."

"Oh yeah," Frankie said less than enthusiastically.

"What do you mean, she got bored?" Cleo asked after she doused her scrambled eggs with ketchup.

"She got tired of me. She thought I was boring."

"Do you think you're boring? I don't find you boring in the least."

"Electra needed a lot of attention, a lot of action, a lot of people around. I'm introverted. I like to spend time alone, writing songs and, you know, thinking about things. After a while, Electra couldn't take it anymore. She said living with me was driving her crazy. She moved out a week later."

"There's nothing wrong with being quiet."

"I'm glad you think so."

Four

"Cleo, why don't you go out with someone?" Alice asked her.

Frankie raised an eyebrow. This ought to be interesting. She stood behind the counter refilling the salt and pepper shakers.

"I came here to get a sandwich, not to get grilled — the sandwich or myself," Cleo responded, smiling at both of them.

"I get so sick of watching Romaine strut her new girlie friend in here while you sit and watch. Doesn't it bother you?"

"Well, I wouldn't call it pleasant. But what am I supposed to do? Move? I like it here, and if that means putting up with Romaine's latest, that's the way it goes. Now can I have my sandwich?"

"I know what your problem is. You're afraid to go out with other women," Alice said, smugly pursing her lips.

"I am not!"

"Ever gone out with another woman?"

"Not exactly."

"You can't count Romaine's leftovers," Alice said, putting her hands on her hips, obviously referring to Bobbi.

"All right, then no, I haven't gone out with other women. It doesn't mean I'm afraid of them. I wouldn't know where to look anyway. I don't like the bar. Besides, that would give Romaine way too much satisfaction having someone tell her that I was desperate and out cruising."

"How about the ads? We're not far from the city. Why not find someone that way?" Alice suggested.

"I've already thought of that, and I've decided that I'm going to advertise."

"That's great. What are you looking for?"

"I've decided that since I don't do well with lesbians, I want a curious bi, no strings attached, petite, attractive femme, discreet, no psycho bitches, no lesbians need apply."

Frankie burst into laughter.

Alice looked at both of them confused.

"What's that supposed to mean?"

"Have you read the ads lately? They're an embarrassment to the lesbian community. It seems all anybody wants these days is a pretty little plaything to show off to their friends and fuck in secret. It's disgusting, and I'd rather grow old alone and have my dignity than subject myself to those new creatures who call themselves lesbians."

"I still say that you're afraid of going out with other women," Alice said, refilling Cleo's coffee.

"All right. Then you find me someone to go out with, and I will go out on one date to prove you wrong."

"I want you to go out with Frankie."

"What!"

"What am I, the bargain date?" Frankie said, screwing up her face.

"No, but you are cute," Cleo replied.

"Is that your attempt at romance?" Frankie replied.

"No, but if you go out with me I won't have to listen to Alice bitch at me anymore. We don't have to kiss or anything."

Frankie looked at her and shook her head. "You know, it's no wonder you don't go out with other women."

"Why? Because I'm basically incompetent?"

"You got it."

"See, Alice, it's not as if I didn't try. Women just don't want to go out with me."

Frankie's pulse quickened. She thought Cleo was crazy, but she found herself oddly attracted to her. It was hard to take seriously someone who wore underwear as an outfit, but Cleo was amusing and easy to be with, and right now Frankie needed a friend.

"It doesn't mean you're hopeless. You need a little coaching. How about I ask you out? Not everyone's a top," Frankie said, knowing she was blushing and wishing she wasn't.

"Okay," Cleo replied good-naturedly.

"Cleo, would you like to go out for a beer and maybe a moonlit walk through the cornfield, say tomorrow night?" Frankie asked, putting her shoulders back trying to appear confident.

"Do I have to get dressed up?"

Alice rolled her eyes. "Just say yes. You *are* hopeless."

"It's a legitimate question," Cleo replied, looking hurt.

"No, you can wear your underwear if you like."

"It's less to take off," Alice said.

Surprised and embarrassed, Cleo and Frankie looked at her. Almost simultaneously they said, "It's not like that."

They smiled at each other, relieved. Maybe this could be fun.

"You still haven't given me your answer," Frankie said.

"All right. I'd love to."

"Good. How about I pick you up Friday at six?" Frankie said.

"I didn't know you had a car," Cleo said.

"Shit! I don't," Frankie replied, feeling stupid. Electra had the Volkswagen they'd bought together. She was supposed to send Frankie the money for her half, but Frankie knew she'd never see it.

"Even though I'm not a top, I'll pick you up."

"Thanks."

"That wasn't hard," Alice said.

"But I know Frankie," Cleo replied.

"So? Lots of women make friends and then find themselves attracted and go out."

"But it's harder because you don't want to wreck the friendship if the dating part doesn't work out," Cleo replied, looking puzzled.

"Must you analyze everything to death? Women get to know each other, they don't become best friends, before they go out. Rather they meet, talk like friends, and then go out. You don't normally walk up to a perfect stranger and say, 'Hey, would you like to go out?' Usually you get to know them a bit, and then you ask them out. I can't believe I'm explaining this to a forty-year-old woman. Where have you been? Never mind. Under the spell of Romaine, lesbian heartbreaker of the world."

"I've never asked anyone out on a date."

Alice looked at Frankie. "For me, teach her a few things will you?"

Frankie smiled at Cleo. "If she'll let me."

Cleo sighed, "I suppose I should get on with my life. Maybe a Princess Charming will come along, kiss me, and break the evil spell."

"What evil spell would that be?" came a voice from the kitchen. Romaine had come in the back. She was carrying three white roses and a package of tea. She sat next to Cleo at the counter. Alice poured her a cup of coffee.

Cleo looked over at her. "The one that keeps me waiting."

Romaine took her hand gently. "I brought you a present to make up for behaving badly the other day."

Cleo took the roses and the tea — orange spice, her favorite.

"Truce?"

"Truce," Cleo replied, looking kindly at Romaine. She did have her sweet moments.

Frankie watched, feeling disgust dotted with a small pang of jealousy. She swatted it away. Cleo wasn't supposed to mean anything to her. It wasn't even a freely chosen date; it had been arranged. But she felt compassion, knowing that Cleo loved Romaine, and she couldn't help herself.

Frankie had been like that once. She'd let Electra mistreat her because she loved her. She had believed the lies, ignored the mysterious disappearances, the money taken, the unaccounted-for long-distance phone calls. She did all that because of love. And their love hadn't covered nearly the span of Romaine and Cleo's.

Romaine and Cleo were leaving together. Cleo looked over her shoulder at Frankie. "Tomorrow night. Don't forget."

"I won't," Frankie replied, clearing away the coffee mugs.

"What's tomorrow night?" Romaine asked.

"Frankie and I are going out on a date," Cleo replied without hesitation.

"How cute," Romaine said, seeing Frankie as no real threat.

Frankie looked back at her. *Don't be too sure. Stranger things have happened.*

Five

Cleo stood in front of the full-length mirror in her cozy dormer bedroom. Even when Romaine lived here, the room retained its dignity. Cleo understood some of Romaine's chagrin over the house. It was her house, and she had no intention of letting Romaine change its essence.

She studied her reflection. She had carefully chosen her best for the occasion. She wore silk paisley boxers and a man's late-Victorian undershirt. Cleo had researched and remade the history of underclothing.

* * * * *

Romaine had hated it when Cleo first wore boxers around the house and then in the fields where she grew the produce for the restaurant.

Romaine had wanted her to manage the restaurant when they bought the old house and converted it. But Cleo was better at carpentry, furniture refinishing, and gardening, so when Alice Montgomery had come to town, Cleo hired her and soon promoted her to manager. The place had made money ever since.

Cleo was forever improving things. The huge field behind the restaurant had grown into a flourishing plot because Cleo had become tired of the constant bickering with the local produce supplier over the poor quality of his wares.

One day Romaine was in the process of guiding the health inspector through the restaurant and grounds. Cleo was in the cage of a Bobcat tearing up the back acre of the property in her boxers and undershirt. Romaine was furious. "How can I conduct business relationships when my partner can't get it together enough to put clothes on?" Cleo acquiesced and wore shorts. It was hot and dirty in the fields.

Cleo was definitely proletariat, whereas Romaine was bourgeoisie. Despite their differences, the produce was a success. Cleo grew every kind of chili, tomato, and other vegetable oddity, and the food was awesome. They were a bona fide success. Their reputation made the city papers, and in fact it was a reporter for the paper whom Cleo had stumbled upon that day at Romaine's studio.

After that Cleo took to wearing underwear on a

regular basis, expanding her collection, beginning her research. When Romaine grew tired of her playmate and came back, Cleo stuck to her wardrobe of choice. When Romaine complained, Cleo reminded her that the boxers were Romaine's punishment for transgression.

Cleo no longer wore regular clothes, but the underwear had definitely improved. Underwear, men's at least, had gotten stylish. The designer labels were the best. Cleo had the best underwear in town. The kids called her Underwear Lady, but since wearing underwear was in vogue the kids mimicked Cleo's style. She had taken underwear to fashion heights.

Surveying herself, Cleo deemed the outfit a success. At forty she was still an attractive woman. She was fit and tanned from working in the fields and taking long hikes. Her sun-streaked blond hair hung lightly on her shoulders. She had a thin nose, high cheekbones, and full lips.

She smiled at herself. *Not bad for an old broad. It's a pity my wife doesn't think so. I should really have an inferiority complex, having been left as many times as I have. Instead I'm crazy, but if I wasn't crazy I'd have murdered Romaine, joined a nunnery, run off to Kathmandu, or committed myself years ago. There really should be a place for lesbians like me, a sanitarium for the sick at heart. Or there could be a group of avengers who sew up the cunts of unfaithful lovers.* Cleo smiled at the thought. *Thank god no one can read minds, or I'd be in deep shit.*

"I'm going on a date," she told Marlowe, the black and gray tabby.

She strolled from the room feeling herself to be the epitome of undergarment fashion. *Calvin, you can't hope to compare.*

Across town Frankie sat on the porch having a gin and tonic with her aunt Ella. Ella was an old butch. She worked in the local lumberyard and had a variety of femme girlfriends. She was a no-nonsense woman interested in the animal pleasures of life: drinking, smoking, and fucking.

"Your mother blames me for your unfortunate choice," Ella said, rolling a cigarette.

"What do you mean?" Frankie asked her.

"Your being a dyke."

"How could that be your fault?"

"Those summers we spent together. She thinks I brainwashed you."

Frankie laughed. "If anything, she's the one who convinced me being straight wasn't where it's at. When she said she didn't understand why I like women, I told her I didn't understand why she likes men. You don't jive in bed, you don't communicate well with each other, and you don't like to do the same things. Why would I want to spend the rest of my life with someone like that? Why settle?"

"Well put. Another cocktail, dear?"

"Sure. I loved my summers with you. They were the best part of the year."

Ella smiled at her, tousled her dark hair, and took her glass.

When Frankie got into Cleo's bright yellow antique truck, she felt tipsy having had three gin and tonics. She looked at Cleo with a silly grin.

Cleo could smell her. "Have you been drinking, young lady?" Cleo asked.

"Why, can you tell?"

"You smell like a juniper tree."

"Sorry. I had a few with Ella while I was waiting. I guess they snuck up on me."

"Don't worry. I won't take advantage of you," Cleo said.

"Shucks," Frankie said, smiling.

"You wouldn't want an old thing like me anyway."

"You're not old. Ella is old."

"She still attracts 'em like flies. In fact, she's slept with some very prominent figures in this town. Head of the garden club, for example. Lots of closet cases."

"I'm thirty-four, you know, that's not exactly a baby."

Cleo would have guessed Frankie to be in her twenties. "No, I guess you're right."

There were two bars in town. When you got thrown out of one, you had another one to go to. By the time you got thrown out of that one, you were allowed back in the first one. It didn't matter which one you frequented since they were both owned by the same couple. Liza and Mel, having worked in dyke bars for years all over the country, had retired in Moroni and started one bar then the other.

Out of the corner of her eye Cleo saw Romaine's shiny black BMW convertible. Romaine could be pretentious at times. The car was one of those pretensions. Cleo wouldn't want a car like that no matter how much money she had, which was another point of contention between them. Cleo was a peasant at heart. She couldn't buy a car that cost that much when other people didn't have a decent place to live, let alone a car of any kind.

Inside Romaine and Cynthia sat at a table across from the dance floor. Cleo nodded at them and guided Frankie to the bar. They each took a stool.

"Want a beer?" Cleo asked.

"I'm supposed to be the top."

"That's right. Let's start over."

"Would you like a beer?" Frankie asked.

"Please, a Tecate with lime."

Frankie looked around while she waited for her order. The large bar was half full. Frankie never would have guessed the town had that many lesbians. She recognized many of the women from various transactions around town and nodded her greeting. The bank teller, the grocery store clerk, the waitress at the five and diner, the Avon lady. Frankie was impressed. Everyone seemed glad to see a fresh face and to know for sure that she was one of them. Frankie might have some friends after all. Maybe being away from her old environs would do her good, make her less jaded.

"You like to play to pool?" Cleo asked her.

"Sure," Frankie said.

They chalked up. Romaine and Cynthia watched. Frankie didn't understand how Romaine could have dumped Cleo for Cynthia. Cleo very attractive with smoldering good looks. Cynthia paled in comparison. It must be the allure and challenge of the new that drew Romaine away.

What Frankie liked most about Cleo was that she was uninhibited and unselfconscious about her looks. She acted as if she wasn't homely, and that was good enough. Sometimes Frankie caught Romaine watching Cleo making a shot, her eyes traveling across Cleo's firm thighs and rear, her intense profile, her strong arms reaching across the table. Frankie thought she saw remorse in Romaine's gaze. *You should have thought of that before you dumped her.*

As if trying to smother those thoughts, Romaine asked Cynthia to dance. Cleo watched them for a second.

"Let's go get a beer," she suggested.

"No, let's dance first," Frankie said. *We'll give Romaine something worry to about.*

"If you insist."

"I do."

Romaine watched as Cleo and Frankie stepped out to the dance floor. When the song was over they stopped. Cleo started to walk off because it was a slow song, but Frankie grabbed her hand.

"Stay."

Cleo did, letting Frankie draw her close, their two bodies moving in synchronicity. They were the same height and fit together nicely. Romaine was taller than Cleo, and she had always felt small in her arms.

When the song was over, Frankie looked at her. "That was okay, wasn't it?"

"It was."

"Not bad for a first date, then?" Frankie said.

"Not bad at all. But what about that moonlit walk in the cornfield?"

"Can't do that until next week. I checked the calendar."

"Does that mean we could do it then? It wouldn't have to be a date or anything."

"You're doing it all wrong." Frankie smiled. "You should have said that I had planned that all along so now you have to go out with me again."

"I just didn't want you to think that you had to go out with me again or anything... Well, you know, Alice arranged this and all."

"Cleo, I had a nice night, and I'd like to be friends. I like talking to you. I like being with you. Okay?"

"Okay."

Cleo walked Frankie up to her door.

"I know I said that you didn't have to kiss me or anything, but could I have a hug?" Cleo asked shyly.

Frankie smiled at her. "Sure."

Cleo held her for a minute, smelling her. She liked the way she smelled, and Frankie didn't pull away. They stood there for a moment holding each other, letting their bodies get to know each other. Cleo let go, and Frankie lightly kissed her cheek.

"You didn't say I couldn't kiss you," Frankie said, hopping up the front stairs.

"No, I didn't."

Six

"How'd the date go?" Alice asked, after the morning breakfast rush died and they had time to breathe again.

Frankie was counting her tips. Soon she would have enough money to buy that motorcycle in front of Earl's Cycles that she was coveting. Each night she put her wad of bills in a coffee can that she kept under her bed. Frankie didn't like banks. She liked the tangible accessibility of hard cash. She hardly heard Alice for the chink of change.

"Well . . . ?" Alice prodded.

"What?" Frankie said.

"The date... last night, remember?"

"Thirty-eight dollars and seventeen cents," Frankie said, looking up. "Oh, the date. The date was fun. Cleo's a good sport."

"She does clean up well," Alice said, gently nudging Frankie.

"She's a pretty lady, not the kind you notice right at first but then..."

"Best kind, sweetie. But don't get your heart set on anything. I've been trying to get her away from Romaine for as long as I can remember. You mark my words. When Romaine snaps her fingers, Cleo'll be right there."

"You really think so?"

"I know so. Seen it happen too many times. One of Romaine's old flames, Bobbi, got in real tight with Cleo. I thought for sure that she could break the spell. She loved Cleo, more than she ever did Romaine, but when push came to shove, Cleo couldn't do it. Romaine wasn't even livin' here then, but Cleo hung around waiting. When Romaine came back, Cleo took her in. I thought it'd about kill Bobbi. Poor thing. She's up in the city now. Just couldn't stand the sight of those two after all that happened. Cleo didn't mean to hurt her, but she's a one-woman woman, even if that particular woman is sleeping with somebody else. Strangest thing. Sad too."

"Being friends seems the safest thing around here anyway," Frankie said, looking away, feeling guilt give her eyes an instant sheen. She didn't want Alice to read anything in her face. She had spent all morning thinking about how Cleo felt in her arms, her strong back, her soft breasts pressed against her.

She knew it was dangerous. It was supposed to be friendly and nothing more, but it felt good to be held again.

After work she walked by Cleo's. She hadn't come into the restaurant that morning, and Frankie missed her.

She stood watching Cleo shovel a large spherical cone of black dirt into a wheelbarrow. Frankie thought about a poem she studied in school, William Carlos Williams's "The Red Wheelbarrow":

*So much depends
upon*

*a red wheel
barrow*

...so much depends on...on a body, what a nice body, Frankie mused. Cleo was wearing her usual underwear, only briefer, Calvin Kleins and a sports bra. Frankie admired her. Cleo was sleek and muscular. With a baseball cap on backward she looked like a young man in his prime.

Strange, how some lesbian bodies don't change like other women's. They stay slim-hipped and taut like a boy's body. Frankie liked firm bodies, though most of her girlfriends had been the voluptuous variety. She seemed to attract that kind of woman. She didn't love them any less, but she craved the toned ones. She wanted to run her hands over tight muscles, watching them flex as the woman moved beneath her ardent touch.

Cleo looked up, her face smeared with black dust. "What are you doing?"

"Watching you. Somebody told me you had a date last night. How was it?"

Cleo smiled and came toward the fence. "It was nice, very nice."

"That's good to hear. So what's up? We missed you at coffee."

"My dirt came today. I couldn't resist — I had to get it down. You want some lemonade?"

"Sure."

Cleo opened the gate.

"Botanical paradise you've got going here. Just can't get enough plant life?"

"Yeah, it keeps me sane."

"What makes you think you're sane?"

Cleo gave her a gentle shove. "Watch it. You'll damage my fragile self-image."

They sat on the back deck sipping lemonade.

"You need some help with the dirt?" Frankie asked, looking at the looming black cone.

"You don't want to do that. It's not fun."

"I don't mind. I like hard work."

"Well... only if you'll stay for dinner. We'll do the barter system — you help me with the dirt, and I'll feed you. You like Mexican food?"

"Yeah."

"Good. I'll make you my famous chili casserole and we'll do cervesas."

"Sounds wonderful."

Frankie rolled up her sleeves, and they set to work. By dinnertime they had reduced the cone to a soft, fluffy, rich carpet that lay across the herb garden Cleo would plant there.

"I'll show you the plants, and you can congratulate yourself for doing the hardest part. Looking at you, I wonder if you're not walking off with some of my precious dirt," Cleo said.

Frankie was dusted in black. "Maybe I should go home and take a shower."

"No, I don't think so. Ella will have you drinking juniper berries again, and I'll lose my dinner companion. You can shower here and borrow an outfit. God knows I have enough of them."

"All forms of underwear?"

"Of course. Now come on, I'll show you the bath and get you some clothes. Are boxers and a T-shirt okay? Or would you prefer knickers or, better yet, I'll pick something out."

"Something flattering, I hope."

"Nothing but."

Cleo was scalding peppers, filling the kitchen with their pungent aroma, when a quick knock sounded at the door and Romaine poked her head in the kitchen.

Cleo looked up. "You know, someday your swift entrances could embarrass us both."

"That'll be the day," Romaine said, smiling. "It smells wonderful in here. Chili casserole?"

"Yes."

"The dirt looks good. God, you got it down fast."

"I had help."

"How was your date?"

"It was nice, very nice. I had a good time. I like

Frankie," Cleo said, smiling at Frankie, who had walked in.

"Cleo, where do you want the towels?"

"Around the corner on the washer. We'll wash your clothes too."

"Such service," Frankie said, smiling as she left the room.

Romaine looked at Cleo with a raised eyebrow. "I'll say the date went well. She's still here."

"She helped me with the dirt. Besides, it's not any of your business. I'm not the one we have to worry about," Cleo retorted.

Frankie returned. Romaine studied her while she tasted the sauce.

"I hope she hasn't got you into the underwear thing too."

Frankie looked like a little prince in her period ensemble, her short hair dangling in wet ringlets, her brisk blue eyes accented by her now bronze skin.

"I'll have you know that those are reproductions of medieval underclothes. The shirt, complete with vents, is from the fifteenth century, and the bottoms are braies, which tie at the knee and come from the same period."

Frankie looked down at herself. She suddenly felt like a museum piece.

Romaine rolled her eyes. "Artistic lingerie. Can't you find something better to do with your time?"

"How I spend my time is my own affair, and I like to sew. It consumes a lot of lonely evenings."

"It looks like you won't be lonely tonight."

"No, I won't. Did you want to stay for dinner? We could make it a threesome," Cleo said diplomatically.

"There's an idea, something we haven't tried," Romaine said, eyeing Frankie lasciviously.

Frankie looked away.

"I didn't mean like that. Dinner, I meant dinner."

"You should have been more specific. No, I told Cynthia we'd go out. God knows the woman can't cook. I do miss your cooking. Cleo's a good cook, Frankie. You're in for a treat. I'd better be going. I was just in the neighborhood and thought I'd stop by. Goodnight, darling," Romaine said, kissing Cleo lightly on the cheek.

Frankie thought she detected a flash of jealousy in Romaine. But if she had, Romaine quickly brushed it away and left.

"Would you like a beer?"

"Please," Frankie replied, finding herself breathing more easily now that Romaine was gone.

"I'm sorry about that."

"About what?"

"Romaine."

"I'm the one who gets to stay for dinner."

"I'm glad," Cleo said, smiling.

Seven

Cleo studied the garden with rapt attention. An organic gardener, she avoided pesticides because they frightened her. She equated chemicals with men, who also frightened her: violent and toxic.

She plucked herbaceous pests from their leafy paradise, washed aphids away with dish soap, and cursed the mysterious ground-hugging flies that danced about her pots, but she refused to douse her insect adversaries with strange-colored powders and obnoxious-smelling sprays. She studied the promises on insecticide labels but never bought them.

She resolved herself to nature's law, survival of the fittest, marveling at the pest resistance of some plants and the quick demise of others. Sometimes the weakened plant would bring itself back, which was a triumph in the battle. The strong plants simply outlasted the onslaught, but the small, weak ones that survived were the heroes. They had less of a chance but still made it.

Cleo learned a lot of things from her garden, nothing tangible enough to explain to another person, but things worth knowing. Romaine thought her crazy for the way she would muck about in the garden, daydreaming, traveling into nature, but she admired her spunk. The only garden Romaine thought worth anything was the plot that grew the produce for the restaurant, the plants that made money.

Cleo often wondered when Romaine looked at the garden if she saw dollar bills basking in the sun or if she saw the plants. Romaine was greedy, and Cleo had never managed to change that. Romaine liked money. She liked to make money, and enough was never enough. She was a true capitalist.

Lost in her thoughts, Cleo was sipping an iced tea when she heard the rumbling of a motorcycle in the drive. When she walked around front, she found Frankie sitting on the shiny orange motorcycle, smiling ear to ear.

"What do you think?"

"It's beautiful," Cleo said, running her hand across the smooth gas tank. "Did you just get it?"

"Yep. You're the first one to see it. Want to go for a ride? I'll be safe."

Cleo smiled. "Okay." Romaine had always said she

was easily influenced by whoever her hanging-out buddy was at the time. Cleo felt like a teenage boy when she was with Frankie, and she kind of liked it. *I can be twelve again,* Cleo thought, hopping on the back of the bike.

"I feel so butch," Cleo shouted over the rumble of the bike.

"I think it needs a muffler."

"Nah. It's a bad-boy bike. Supposed to be that way."

"Okay. But are you willing to pay my tickets when Heinous Harry gets a load of it?"

"I might. I wouldn't worry about it. Ella's slept with his wife. You won't get any tickets."

They rode across town and showed Ella the bike.

She came out in her overalls, checked it over, and nodded her approval.

"You'll definitely get the girls with a machine like that. I might have to borrow it sometime. You two look good on it," Ella said. Frankie gave her a look, but Ella just smiled coyly.

Frankie had told her every time she asked about the two of them that they were friends and nothing more.

Cleo smiled at her. "Let's go up to the Peaks."

"Yeah," Frankie said, catching her excitement.

"You gals be careful. That's a mighty winding road," Ella said.

Cleo loved the way the wind felt on her body as they rode up the hill. She closed her eyes and held on tight to Frankie, who touched her hand sometimes to see if she was all right. It felt nice to touch. They hadn't since the first night. It seemed touching might mean something.

It was twilight when they reached the top. They sat on the ridge and watched the sun set over the town.

"Do you see my house?"

"Where?" Frankie asked.

"Over there." Cleo pointed. "And there's the restaurant and there's Romaine's studio. Sometimes I wish it was on the other side of Baskum Hill so I wouldn't have to see it."

"Does it ruin the view?"

"Most times it does."

"And what time doesn't it?"

"The times when she's being decent, when I think she might love me enough to stay."

"Isn't it hard when she comes back not to think of the bad times?" Frankie asked, not looking at Cleo as she scratched the dry orange dirt with a stick.

"Yes, but Romaine has a way of making me forget. The past is the past, and since she has no sense of remorse I've given up trying to make her feel bad. We pick up where we left off, which is why we keep failing. We probably need counseling. But Romaine wouldn't take five paces into a therapist's office. So we fail again and again."

"Do you think you might ever fall in love with someone else?"

"I don't know. It would be a good thing. I think if I did it might make Romaine move on too. One of us really should stop this cycle. I haven't found the right person to fall in love with, so I end up having friends but no lovers."

"Not even Bobbi?"

"Two souls tainted by Romaine does not a love affair make."

"But you two were friends?"

"Good friends."

"Do you think it would ruin a friendship if you fell in love with someone not tainted by Romaine?"

"I think it would depend on how the other person felt, if she felt the same way. Sometimes it's a good thing that your lover is your best friend, and maybe Alice is right. Falling in love is a logical extension of that. I was never friends with Romaine first."

"I was never friends with Electra either."

"Hmm," Cleo said.

"Do you think we learned anything?"

"I don't know, but I hope so."

Studying the sky, Frankie said, "It's getting dark. We should go." The moon was full and coming into view.

They drove back toward town. Frankie stopped at Jenkins's cornfield.

"What's up?" Cleo asked.

"It's a full moon, and I promised you a moonlit walk through the cornfield."

"You did. Let's go. It is a beautiful night."

"Wait," Frankie said, taking Cleo's hand and guiding her to one row of corn and herself to the other. They could barely see each other in the dark, thick rows of corn.

"Take off your clothes."

"What!"

"You heard me. It's a naked moonlit walk. Come on. I can't see you. It'll be fun," Frankie said, taking off her shoes and letting her toes sink into the soft earth.

"All right, but you didn't tell me about this part," Cleo said, taking off her shirt and knickers.

"No, I didn't."

At first it felt odd walking outside naked, and then it felt sensuous. Cleo caught glimpses of Frankie's flesh through the corn. They laughed and ran, weaving their way through the corn. They were breathing hard as they reached the end of the field.

When they stopped to catch their breath, Cleo looked up and saw Jenkins, his shotgun cradled in his arms.

"I want you out of my field now!" his thick voice boomed.

Cleo and Frankie took off running. When they reached the other side they laughed hysterically as they got dressed.

"It's going to be all over town tomorrow," Cleo said, wiping the tears from her eyes with the corner of her shirt.

"Oh no. It wasn't supposed to be like this. What was he doing out there anyway?"

"I don't know. He probably heard the corn rustling and came out looking for vandals," Cleo said.

"Instead all he got was two naked women."

Cleo grabbed her hand. "Thank you, that was fun."

"I don't know if you'll think so tomorrow when everyone gives you queer looks."

"Worse things have happened."

Eight

It was Cleo's turn to play prep cook, only because Emmanuel, the restaurant's latest prep cook, was too hung over to chop veggies. Cleo sent him home after he vomited in the dish sink. She was an understanding sort, but she made him forfeit his next day off. He limped home, and she began prepping for lunch. Cleo liked to chop food. It allowed her time to muse. Right now she was musing about Frankie. She found herself doing that a lot lately. Did it mean something? Maybe it did. Her musing was interrupted by the clink of boots on the gray tile floor. She looked up. It was Romaine.

Romaine picked up a small carrot and bit it in half.

"Rumor has it that Jenkins almost shot two trespassers last night. Seems you and your young friend were naked little nymphs trotting through the corn," Romaine said, pointing the carrot at Cleo.

Cleo looked at her and smiled. "At least he didn't shoot us."

"True. You would have been forced to pick rock salt out of each other's asses. That might not have been so unpleasant. What's the deal with you two?"

"I don't think that's any of your business, Romaine."

"Are you two sleeping together?"

"Why do you want to know?"

"What's the big deal? Either you are or you aren't."

"The big deal is that my love life is none of your concern. I don't ask you anything about Cynthia, even though I know you were fucking under my roof for a time. I could have asked, but I didn't."

"If you asked I would tell."

"No, you wouldn't."

"Try me."

"Okay. Is she a good fuck?"

"She is, but she's stingy."

"I don't want to know this."

"You asked."

"You forced me."

"I wonder what other things I could force you to

do," Romaine said, pressing Cleo against the table, holding her shoulders, looking into her eyes. "I miss you, Puddle."

"You only miss me when you're fucking someone else. I'm always sweeter then."

"And you are sweet," Romaine said, spreading Cleo's legs with her knee.

"Romaine, let me go. We can't do this anymore."

"Why not? It wouldn't be the first time. Maybe what we need is for you to forever remain the mistress."

"What we need to do is learn to let go and stop hurting each other and the people who get caught in the middle."

Romaine sighed and looked deep into Cleo's eyes, reassuring herself that love still lurked there. She bent down and kissed Cleo's neck, burying her face in Cleo's sweet smell.

Cleo closed her eyes and let herself be held, remembering how it felt to be loved, a selfish luxury.

The crashing of plates snapped her back from her daydream. Both women turned.

"I'm sorry. I didn't mean to intrude," Frankie said, as she bent to scoop up pieces of broken plates. "I'm so clumsy."

"I'll get a broom," Cleo said.

Romaine knelt next to Frankie. "Remember, whatever is happening between you two, you're no match for me," Romaine said as she fixed her eyes on Frankie.

Frankie looked away. She could feel tears begin to form. She willed them away. *Cleo's not yours, remember,* she told her aching heart as she watched Romaine stand up and walk out.

"You've cut yourself," Cleo said, coming back into the room.

Frankie looked at the blood on the floor and stood up.

"You're shaking. What did she say to you?"

"Nothing."

"I'm sorry," Cleo said, leading Frankie to the sink.

"Sorry about what?"

"You know, Romaine," Cleo said, looking away.

"That's none of my business and, besides, it's inevitable anyway, isn't it?"

"What's inevitable?" Cleo said as she started to bandage Frankie's hand.

"Your getting back with Romaine."

Cleo studied her face for a moment; their eyes locked.

Frankie wanted to scream. *I love you, dammit! I want you more than she ever did. You're all I ever think of, and the thought of never having you is driving me crazy. I won't break your heart. I would never hurt you like that. I would hold you so close and so tender that you'd never be sad or scared or lonely again. If I could have you I wouldn't* want *anyone else.* Swallowing her hurt and her rage, she looked away to hide the pain in her eyes.

Cleo took her hand, touched her cheek tenderly. "Not necessarily."

Her answer surprised them both. Frankie smiled weakly, wishing it was true.

"Besides, Romaine would never walk naked through a cornfield with me."

"Yeah, but we're the talk of the town," Frankie said, squeezing Cleo's hand.

"In more ways than one, I'm sure."

Later, Frankie's words kept clouding Cleo's head. *It's inevitable, isn't it?*

Does it have to be? What makes me think I'm strong enough to break a twenty-year habit? And how would I ever convince Romaine that it really is over? That I have to move on? She's already going through the motions of winning me back. Do I have the determination, the will, to stave her off? Or will I fall? I always fall so willingly into her arms when I get to the point of craving her like a junkie needing a fix. Can I kick my habit to fall in love with someone who might really love me? Cleo covered her head with a pillow and groaned. Marlowe rubbed against her arm.

Cleo removed the pillow and looked at the cat, scratching her ears. "You've been a better, more steadfast companion than Romaine ever was. Dammit, this time I'm gonna try. I wish I could just call Frankie and tell her that I need her here, that I need her patience. I need her to teach me to love again. Frankie, break the spell." Cleo eyed the phone and then shut off the light. *I am a coward. Providence, save me from myself.*

She spent days having conversations with herself

and Marlowe, trying to figure out how she felt about Romaine and how she felt about Frankie. Most of the time she came up with a knot in her stomach and a queer look on her face.

One afternoon Romaine caught her in the middle of one of her one-sided conversations.

"What's wrong?" Romaine said, climbing up to the porch.

"Nothing," Cleo said.

"You're lying. You're not a good liar."

"I should be after all those years of living with you."

"It's a trait you're born with. You can't learn it. Besides, it's not a good thing."

"Now, there's a change of heart," Cleo said, studying Romaine's eyes.

"Have you been avoiding me?"

"Why would I be avoiding you?"

"Are you angry with me about the other day... in the kitchen with Frankie?"

"Just because you might have ruined my one chance at happiness?"

Romaine looked away and swallowed hard. "Did I always make you sad?"

Cleo felt an instant pang. "No, sometimes you made me very happy. I'm not avoiding you. I need some space. I need to think about some things."

"Like what?"

"Where my life is going."

"You're not going through the change, are you?"

"No. Now get out of here. I've a million chores to attend to."

"So you're okay?"

"I'm fine."

They looked at each other for a moment. Then Romaine turned. "I love you," she said.

"I know you do. You just have a funny way of showing it."

Nine

"So now that you've got a set of wheels you're not leaving any time soon, are you?" Cleo asked Frankie.

"Why? Would you miss me?" Frankie asked, dodging Cleo's rather intrusive left jab. Frankie was teaching Cleo to box, and Cleo was teaching Frankie to waltz.

"I might," Cleo said, stopping the shadowboxing and grabbing Frankie to draw her close.

"Holding," Frankie said, trying to worm free.

"No, I would miss you. I would really miss you," Cleo said, looking deep into her eyes.

Cleo had thought about it a lot lately but didn't have a point of reference for how she was feeling. She knew she was fond of Frankie, but there was something else too, something she hadn't felt before except with Romaine — sexual energy, a sense of accumulating desire. She wanted Frankie in ways she hadn't wanted anyone else. The idea scared her, but at the same time she couldn't stop flirting with it. The thought of Frankie leaving made Cleo hurt. She needed to do something soon, but she wasn't sure what.

"I'm not leaving," Frankie said, brushing Cleo's hair back from her face.

"Will you go to the picnic with me?"

"The annual Pride picnic?"

"Yes."

"Are you asking me out?"

"I guess I am. Will you be my date?"

"Because you want me or because I'm convenient?"

"Oh what a wicked woman! That deserves a noogie," Cleo said.

Frankie broke free. "No, no noogies. I hate noogies! We're too old for that." She ran into the living room. Cleo tackled her on the couch.

"Noogies have no age limit," Cleo said, rubbing her knuckles into Frankie's head.

"No, no, stop!"

"You make the best playmate," Cleo said, thinking that Romaine never played with her. Everything had to be such a grown-up game. "Apologize then."

"For what?"

"For saying that you were convenient. I like you. I like being with you. I invited you because I wanted to spend the day with you."

Frankie looked up at her. "I'm sorry. I'd love to go. Now let me up, you're squashing me."

Cleo quickly kissed her cheek and let her go.

As Frankie lay in bed later that night, she thought about that kiss. She wondered if maybe Cleo felt something for her as well. Maybe she wasn't the only one falling in love. This scared her more than her own knowledge that she was in love. Hers she could hide; Cleo's she could not. When Romaine found out, that would be the end. She would snatch Cleo back so fast... Frankie swallowed hard, knowing it was going to hurt, knowing there was nothing she could do to stop it.

"So you're going to the picnic with Cleo?" Alice asked her the next day as they set up for lunch.

"Who told you that?" Frankie asked, instantly panicked that Cleo would think she was blabbing things all over town.

"Cleo did, and she seemed quite pleased with herself."

"She did?"

"Yes, and you're lucky. Cleo never goes to the picnic when she's not with Romaine. I'd say she thinks you're mighty special. You two sure have gotten on well. Is there something I should know?" Alice chided, raising an eyebrow.

Frankie turned to look at her. "Alice, I'm in love with her, and I've never even kissed her."

"Oh honey, now I warned you about that. Cleo's no good there. When Romaine is done..."

"I know. But can't there be one time when it doesn't happen, one time when it'll be different?"

Alice looked at her for a moment. Frankie was everything Romaine wasn't. She was sincere, honest, easygoing, and talented. Frankie was a musician and wrote beautiful songs. You'd never hear them on the radio, but you'd hear them in your head for hours after she played. And these past few months she'd never seen Cleo so happy. Maybe that was why Romaine was worried.

Alice knew Romaine was worried because she religiously quizzed Alice on Cleo's doings. Romaine thought she was being sly, but Alice knew better.

"What am I going to do, Alice?"

"Leave town," Alice blurted. She regretted it a second later.

Frankie slumped down on a stool and buried her head in her arms, groaning.

"No, no, honey, I didn't mean it. Ah shucks, I was just kidding."

Frankie looked up. "No, you weren't."

Alice sighed and put her hands on her hips, her thinking stance. She waited, then asked, "What do you think Cleo feels?"

"I don't know. I get mixed signals."

"Have you asked?"

"Asked her what?"

"If she has feelings for you."

"I can't do that."

Alice sighed again. "I know you can't. I don't know what to tell you. Pray. Pray Romaine goes away. Pray Cleo stops loving her. Pray you stop feeling this way."

That night Frankie prayed. She didn't know which of the evils to pray for, so she prayed for the love to figure it out and let her know.

Ten

Frankie sat on the bed, watching Cleo finish dressing.

"Will Romaine be there?"

"Yes, darling. Does that make you nervous?" Cleo asked, sitting down to put her shoes on.

"A little. Romaine is rather formidable."

"Don't worry. I won't let her do anything formidable to you. What did she say to you that day you cut your hand?"

"I'll never tell."

"We'll see about that," Cleo said, straddling her and pinning her to the bed. "Torture."

"You can't do that. We're grown-ups," Frankie replied, thinking of the countless times her brother had done the same thing to her.

"So? Torture is a grown-up construct. Are you going to talk?"

"My lips are sealed. It wasn't a big deal. Really."

"It must have been something or you wouldn't think her *formidable*."

Cleo started in, and Frankie squirmed beneath her.

"Cleo, come on."

"Tell me then."

Cleo was strong. Frankie wrestled to no avail.

"All right, all right. She said that I was no competition for her, so I'd better watch it."

Cleo rolled off her, propping herself up on one elbow. "She's got a lot of nerve. You have her worried," she said.

"Why?"

"Because she knows I like you."

"So am I a pawn that you two use to hurt each other?"

Cleo looked at her with hurt in her eyes. Frankie instantly wished she hadn't said it.

"No, darling, given the chance you might find I'm falling in love with you," Cleo said, swallowing hard. She had deemed today the day for letting Frankie know that she wanted her for more than a friend. She had lain in bed last night thinking about how she smelled, how she smiled, how it felt to touch her. She found herself craving that touch.

Frankie sat up and looked at the floor. "Whose chance? Yours or Romaine's?"

"I believe it's up to providence. We'll have to wait and see," Cleo replied, concerned. This scene wasn't in her daydream script.

"See if Romaine comes back?"

"No, see if I take her back."

"That's a given, isn't it?"

"No, not this time. Stop looking so gloomy," Cleo said, getting up and grabbing Frankie's hand, lifting her from the bed. Cleo pulled her close.

Frankie melted into her arms.

"There now, do you feel better?" Cleo asked, running her hand across Frankie's cheek. She lightly kissed her, letting her lips linger. Cleo grabbed Frankie's hand to drag her in the direction of the park.

"Come on. We'll be late for the potato-sack race."

Cleo and Frankie won the race and were recouping on the blanket beneath a tree. Frankie was telling her stories and sucking on a long strand of green wheat. Cleo lay on her side, admiring her profile. Frankie finished and began to tickle Cleo's face with the blossoming end of the grass. She traced her lips, then her neck, and was about to take it a step further when Cleo reached out to kiss her. Someone picked that moment to kick her sandal. Romaine, with Cynthia. Frankie blushed. Cleo sat up and, for the first time since Frankie had known her, looked perturbed.

"What?"

Romaine was taken aback. She quickly recovered.

"We want you guys to come sit with Alice and the rest of the group. The drag queens will be on shortly. I know you like them, and I didn't want you to miss the show."

"Where are you sitting?" Cleo asked.

"On the left side of the grandstand. Are you coming?"

"In a minute," Cleo said. "We'll meet you there."

"All right," Romaine said, taking Cynthia's hand and carting her off.

"I think you upset her," Frankie queried.

"Paybacks are hell," Cleo said, picking up the blanket and shaking it. "Besides she was rude."

Cleo wrapped the blanket around Frankie's shoulders and picked up the picnic basket. Frankie began to walk off.

"Wait, we were about to do something before we were interrupted," Cleo said, pulling on the blanket, drawing Frankie near. Frankie went weak. Cleo kissed her softly, deeply, ardently. This was no friendly kiss. This was a lover's kiss.

"It won't be today or tomorrow, but it'll be soon. I know I ask a lot from you, but if you're willing to wait, I'd like to give us a try," Cleo said, swallowing hard.

"I'll wait. I'd wait for you forever," Frankie blurted.

They stood holding each other. Cleo took her hand and led her to the grandstand. Frankie was in heaven. She was in love, and it was all right.

* * * * *

Romaine turned around, saw them kiss, saw them stand in rapture. She pushed sunglasses up to cover her tears. Cynthia took her hand, but Romaine pulled back. She looked away and never saw the hurt in Cynthia's eyes, never heard the whispered apology.

Eleven

Frankie went around to pick up Cleo. A strange car was in the driveway. Cleo heard Frankie's bike and came outside, folding her arms across her chest.

"What's wrong?" Frankie asked.

"It's Romaine," Cleo answered.

"Is she here?" Frankie asked, knowing that Romaine drove an expensive sports car of some sort, curious if this was the one.

"No, Cynthia is."

"I don't understand," Frankie said, putting her

hands in her back pockets, beginning to wonder why they weren't having this conversation inside.

"Tonight Romaine told Cynthia that she needed some space, some time alone."

"In other words, piss off," Frankie said.

Cleo nodded. "Needless to say, she's not taking it well."

"But what is she doing here?"

"She needed to talk to someone," Cleo said matter-of-factly.

"What does that have to do with you?"

"I'm the only one who can begin to fathom Romaine's unusually cruel behavior."

"She stole your wife. Why would you want to have anything to do with her?"

"Someone has to help. I've been there. I know what it feels like. They always run to me," Cleo said, looking past her.

Frankie felt her jaw tighten. She hated how Romaine ruled over everything like some viper queen. *She's an addiction these women can't get past, including Cleo. Why doesn't one of them tell her to fuck off and take a good long walk, preferably in front of a fast-moving train?* Frankie thought glumly. *Romaine always wins.*

"Do you clean up all her messes?"

"Someone has to," Cleo replied.

"No one helped you."

"Yes, someone did."

"Who?"

"You."

Frankie looked away.

"Don't be angry. I can't leave Cynthia alone. It's

bad. She loves Romaine, and she doesn't understand why this is happening."

"I'm not angry. I'm disappointed," Frankie said.

Cleo took her hand. "I'll make it up to you. I promise."

Frankie looked at her and kissed her savagely, a kiss of possession. She got on her bike without saying a word.

Cleo watched her ride off. She went back inside and poured Cynthia a brandy, handing her the box of tissues.

Fucking Romaine. How can she be so cruel? Cleo thought, as she sipped her brandy and waited for Cynthia to compose herself. *She makes all of us fall in love with her and then she turns our love, faith, and devotion back on us to taunt and torment. Our emotional landscapes become naked, raw hurt. We turn to one another to dress wounds that only a beloved can truly heal. Love, the best and most devious of human games.*

"Is it me? Is it something I've done?" Cynthia looked up.

"No, it's her."

"What does she want?"

"I wish I knew. I wish someone knew."

"What am I going to do?"

"Stay away for as long as you can."

"What will that do? She's all I ever think about. I love her. Can't she see that?"

"Romaine only sees what she wants to. She's frightened that you have feelings for her, so she runs. She does it every time."

"What am I supposed to do? Pretend I don't?"

"If you want her to stay interested."

"I can't fucking believe this," Cynthia said, tears building.

Cleo held her hand, cursing the day Romaine was born.

The next day Cleo brought Frankie a present. Frankie was at the counter of the café when Cleo walked in holding a white daylily and a small package.

"This is for yesterday, for spoiling our night," Cleo said, holding out the peace offering. "I'm sorry."

Frankie blushed. "You don't have to be sorry. I didn't mean to be angry with you."

Cleo shrugged. "Open it."

Inside the small box was a leather pouch and seven polished stones, each one different.

"Whenever you have a moment in your life, one you'll never forget, good or bad, put one of the stones in the pouch. When you've put them all in the pouch, you'll have learned everything you need to know to live a life of harmony."

"Thank you," Frankie said, studying the stones. The purple amethyst would be the first stone to go in the pouch. It would be the moment she told Cleo she loved her.

"Is she all right?" Frankie asked, feeling a rush of guilt for being angry with Cynthia in her moment of need.

"She'll live, like we all do. Will you come for dinner tonight?"

"Is this another date?" Frankie asked, smiling.

"Yes, this is a date," Cleo said, taking her hand.

"You're getting better at this, you know."

"I know, thanks to you," Cleo said, smiling.

Twelve

Romaine stood outside the screen door, peering in. "Cleo are you there?" she called out.

Cleo, fresh from the shower, came to the door in her white bathrobe, her hair dripping.

"I'm sorry to barge in, but I need to talk to you," Romaine said, looking suddenly disconcerted, her habitually cool exterior unusually disheveled.

Cleo opened the door.

"What's wrong?"

"Did Cynthia come here last night?"

"Yes. You got what you wanted, obviously."

"What?"

"Breaking it off. She's distraught, and you're free. Do you want a beer?" Cleo said, pulling two cold ones from the fridge.

"Please," Romaine said, taking the beer. "Cleo, I'm not doing well. I don't know what to do. I miss you. I know I treated you bad. I treated Cynthia bad. I don't know what's wrong with me. I feel so disconnected."

Cleo looked right at her. "Romaine, you're selfish. You think only of what you want and not how the consequences of your actions will affect other people, especially the ones stupid enough to love you."

Romaine burst into tears. In twenty years Cleo had seen her cry only three times.

Cleo came over to hold her. "Shhh, don't cry. I didn't mean to be so harsh."

"You're right. That's how I am. I'm a miserable bitch."

Cleo sat on the stool next to her, took her hand. "C'mon, it can't be that bad. You need to spend some time alone and think about what you're doing. Do you really want to let her go?"

Romaine took a drink of beer. "I don't know. I feel as if I'm losing you, and it's driving me crazy. I don't want to lose you, Puddle."

Cleo looked at her, sadness in her eyes.

"Then why do you leave me?"

"I don't know."

"You love me best when you're not with me. Shouldn't that tell you something?"

"Like what?"

"You desire what you don't possess. Romaine, you'll never find happiness that way."

"Are you happy?"

Cleo took a moment to think. "Yes, I am. For the first time in a long while, I'm happy."

"It's because of *her,* isn't it?"

"Yes," Cleo said, looking out the kitchen window.

"You love her, don't you?" Romaine said, tears building in her dark eyes. "You do don't you?"

Cleo wiped her tears away. "I love you, have always loved you, will love you until the day I die, but I can't keep waiting. I can't keep hoping that one day you'll stop hurting me. I love Frankie, and I'd like to try being with her."

Romaine sobbed in Cleo's arms.

Cleo was surprised. "Why are you so upset? You're the one who left me. Remember?"

Romaine looked up, teary eyed. "That doesn't mean I ever stopped loving you."

Cleo got them both another beer. "You are unbelievable. What makes you think you can yank me around like a rag doll that you can put away when you finish throwing it around the room?"

"I don't think that," Romaine pleaded.

"That's how you act. I finally have a chance to find happiness, fidelity, someone to get old with, and now you've realized you made a mistake. It's too late, Romaine. You should have thought of this years ago before you went off fucking other people."

"I didn't know you'd fall in love. You never do."

"No, I always wait. This time I'm not going to."

"Cleo, don't do this!"

"Do what? Do what you always do to me? Romaine, has it ever occurred to you what it was like finding out that you were sleeping around on me? How do you think it felt when I found you and that blond bimbo in bed, in our bed? What do you think that did to my heart? Every time you cheated on me, you chipped away at a little more of my love. Don't be surprised if I don't fall in love with you again. Lord knows, I've done it enough times. This time, I'm the one who's leaving," Cleo said, walking out of the house.

Cleo was halfway across town before she realized she was in her bathrobe and that she'd walked out of her own house.

Romaine was astounded. She left quickly, locking herself in her studio, answering the door to no one.

Frankie opened the front door.

"I know about the underwear thing, but are you moving into a new phase? Bathrobes and, it appears, nothing underneath. You could get arrested for that," Frankie teased.

Cleo didn't smile.

"Come inside. What's wrong?" Frankie asked, alerted to the crisis.

"Nice bathrobe," Ella called out from her recliner, looking up from the sports section.

"Thank you," Cleo said.

"What's wrong?"

Cleo sat at the kitchen table.

"Romaine came over. She's upset because she thinks I'm in love with you, and now she wants me back. She's afraid she's losing me."

Frankie sat quiet for a minute.

"Is she losing you?"

"She lost me a long time ago. But I never had a reason to leave before."

"And now you do?"

Cleo's face got red. "Do I look incompetent? Do I look so stupid that I'm incapable of love? Is it impossible that I might love you? I give up! I don't understand any of you!" Cleo said, marching from the room and letting the screen door slam behind her. Frankie was the second woman in a half an hour that she had left dumbstruck.

Ella came into the room.

"What was that about?"

"I think she loves me," Frankie said quietly.

"Is that how she usually shows it? Comes marching across town in her robe, screams at you, and then leaves?"

"I don't know."

"Do you love her?"

"Yes, I love her. I love her to the point of obsession."

"Then what are you doing sitting here? Go after her," Ella said, smiling.

Frankie flew from the room. She caught up with Cleo on Elm Street.

"Cleo wait! I'm sorry, I'm so sorry," Frankie pleaded.

Cleo had calmed down and was feeling sheepish. She hadn't meant to be so harsh.

She took Frankie in her arms and held her. They were both shaking. She looked deep into her eyes.

"I love you," Cleo said.

"I'm glad," Frankie said.

"Can we go back to your house? I'm afraid Romaine will be at mine."

"Sure," Frankie said, taking her hand and leading her home.

"Can I borrow some clothes? I really do feel ridiculous in my robe. Eccentrics the town will tolerate, nutcases they do not," Cleo said, pulling her robe in tight.

Frankie had never seen Cleo in clothes; neither had Ella. She looked good in a pair of jeans and a shirt.

"Do you have any regular clothes?" Ella asked her, over their sloe gin fizzes. They were sitting on the porch.

"Not really. Haven't bought any for years. But these aren't so bad. I might have to get me some new duds."

Thirteen

Cleo didn't mean to hurt Romaine when she went shopping and bought new ensembles. She was finished with her underwear phase. That was all. But the clothes episode sent Romaine around the bend. Romaine saw it as betrayal. And she held Frankie accountable.

"What's the deal with the clothes anyway?" Romaine asked, eating a radish she had neatly plucked from the salad bowl.

"I simply felt like a change," Cleo responded, stuffing manicotti noodles for dinner.

"Is *she* coming over for dinner?"

"If by *she* you mean Frankie, then yes. Ella is coming too. You're more than welcome to stay. Why don't you call Cynthia and see if she wants to come over? There's plenty."

Romaine leaned her elbows on the counter and peered at Cleo.

"She's still mad at me for wanting some space."

"Romaine, do you love her or is she another plaything?"

Romaine was quiet for a moment. Then she sighed.

"I think in my own weird and psychotic way I do love her. Not like I love you, but I am very fond of her."

"Does she know that?"

"I've never told her. I wouldn't know how to explain it. I know that she loves me, but she doesn't understand me."

"Romaine, no one understands you. It's impossible."

"That's not nice. I always thought you understood me."

"I don't. You only think that because your selective memory is charming you again."

"I like to be charmed," Romaine said, taking Cleo by the waist and waltzing her across the kitchen.

"I miss dancing with you. I miss those other things too," Romaine said, kissing her cheek.

Cleo protested and pulled away, but Romaine held her and kissed her again, more forcibly, until Cleo succumbed.

"I miss you, Cleo," Romaine said. "And I can't

make myself stop loving you. Can't we try just one more time, please?"

Cleo looked at her, feeling sadness rise up. *If only I could trust you. If only I could make myself forget all the times you've hurt me.* "You have driven me to the brink of madness and back. You've hurt me more times than I care to remember, and still I love you, will always love you. But this time is different."

"Different? Different because you're in love with someone else?"

"Yes. How many times did you think you could run away and expect me to wait? Romaine, I'm done waiting."

"What if I'm not done loving you? What if I can't make myself stop loving you? Cleo, I want you back," Romaine said, moving closer.

"I'm not coming back."

"You can say that, but I know better," Romaine said, pressing her up against the counter. She nestled between thighs she now longed for. She started to unbutton Cleo's shirt.

"Dammit, Romaine, I'm not one of your playthings. Don't treat me like one," Cleo said, trying to get away. Romaine held her tight.

"You want me. I know you do. Don't play coy with me. I know you miss me," Romaine said, kissing her and continuing her pursuit.

The doorbell rang.

"Let me go!"

"All right, don't get ruffled."

Cleo answered the door, her face red and her demeanor flustered. Frankie noticed immediately.

"What's wrong?"

"Nothing," Cleo said, smiling at her and kissing her cheek. "Come in. Are you hungry? Hi, Ella, I've got the gin and tonics chilling."

"What a gal," Ella said, patting her shoulder.

Frankie saw Romaine standing in the kitchen doorway. Suddenly, she understood what was bothering Cleo.

"Hello, Romaine. What a lovely surprise. Haven't seen you in a while. How have you been?" Ella asked her.

"Fine, Ella. I'm doing just fine," Romaine said, smiling. She watched Frankie stiffen.

"Why don't you pour drinks, Romaine," Cleo said, "and we'll have them on the deck."

"Certainly," Romaine said, making herself at home. "Shall I set another plate?"

"Since you're staying," Cleo said.

She led them out back. She whispered to Frankie, "I'm sorry."

Frankie looked at her. "Somehow, I don't think this is your doing."

"It's not."

"I missed you," Frankie said, taking her hand.

"I missed you too. How did it go?"

"It was okay," Frankie said. She had gone to the city to make a demo tape.

"I'm glad you went. I know you don't go in for those things. I'm proud of you."

"I'm playing in Rock Springs next week. Will you come?"

"I'd love to."

"Love to what?" Romaine interjected, handing them both a drink.

"Watch her play in Rock Springs," Cleo replied.

"Sounds like fun. You are quite popular at the restaurant. Just the other day Jack the poet complained to me about people's less than enthusiastic response to his work. He seems to think that you've spoiled them," Romaine said, smiling at Frankie.

"Yep. She'll be famous one day and won't hang out with the likes of us. She'll be consorting with those, what do you call them, celebrity dykes?" Ella said, sitting back in a chair and propping up her feet.

"*Celesbos*," Frankie replied.

"Yep, before you know it she'll be one of those," Ella said.

"I doubt that," Frankie replied. "I just like to write songs. I don't go in for the rest."

"Sometimes you don't have a choice in those matters. The press gets a hold of you — " Romaine said.

"And the next thing you know you're sleeping with a reporter, and then you're all over the papers," Cleo said.

Romaine scowled at her, and Ella laughed heartily.

Frankie looked over at Ella, who wiped the tears from her eyes.

"Well, honey, if the shoe fits," Ella replied, looking over at Romaine.

Romaine recovered herself. "My best advice to you would be not to sleep with reporters. They can certainly mess up your life."

"Speaking of reporters, where is your little scribbler?" Ella asked.

"At home pouting," Romaine replied.

"What naughty thing did you do this time?" Ella asked.

"It's more like what didn't I do," Romaine replied.

"I've been there a time or two. Women. Can't live with them, can't live without them. There's no telling," Ella said, finishing her drink.

Frankie went to refill it. Cleo followed to refill her own. Tonight was supposed to be fun, and now it was turning tedious. Cleo had forgotten how Romaine dominated everything.

She looked over at Frankie. "Do you think they'd notice if we just slipped out the front and went out for dinner?"

Frankie walked over and held her. "What's wrong?"

"She's fucking with my life again. I can feel it, and it's not fair to you. I can't expect you to put up with her shit," Cleo said, feeling depression creep in.

Frankie looked deep into her eyes. "This may come as a surprise, but I'm in for the duration. So if you think I'm going to walk away because things get a little sticky, you're much mistaken."

Cleo held her tightly. Frankie kissed her gently at first and then deeper, wanting her right there, wanting to take her, feeling the weight of her body, kissing her everywhere. Cleo felt herself succumbing, forgetting about dinner, her guests, Romaine. Frankie kissed her neck and shoulders and started to unbutton her shirt when they heard a small cough behind them. Ella had come to retrieve her drink.

"If you two'd like, I could take Romaine out to dinner," Ella said, smiling.

Cleo blushed, and Frankie tried to collect herself as they rejoined the others.

"No, no. It's almost ready," Cleo said.

"Good, I'm perfectly starving," Romaine said. "Are you all right? You're flushed." She touched Cleo's cheek. Her color had risen and she looked shaken.

"Yes, I'm fine," Cleo said, turning away.

Romaine looked at Frankie and poured herself another drink. Tonight seemed to be one for drinking. Halfway through dinner they cracked open a third bottle of wine. The wine eased the tension, and by the end of dinner Romaine and Cleo were telling stories about their early days.

"My god, you guys were awful," Frankie said.

"We were," Cleo said. Looking across the table at Romaine, she thought, *If you had known how to control yourself we would be together right now, proudly telling people how long we'd been together. Instead, we're alone, and all we have left is funny stories.* Romaine caught her eye.

Ella got up, "I hate to be the party poop, but early mornings are killers."

"She's right," Frankie said, "Alice in those bright orange pantsuits is difficult enough, but with a hangover..."

Cleo smiled at her. "I'll walk you out," she said, taking Frankie's hand.

Romaine cringed. She'd not seen Cleo with another woman and it hurt. She bit her lip. *I'm losing her. I can't believe I'm losing her.* She felt panic rising up and the sickness of loss covering her like a clammy fog.

"I'll see you in the morning," Cleo said, kissing Frankie goodnight.

"Thanks again, Cleo," Ella said, leading Frankie off.

"She'll be all right," Ella said when she caught Frankie looking back. "They have a past, but Romaine has done things even a kindhearted woman like Cleo can't forgive or forget. Those two might be friends and sisters, but they're done being lovers."

"You think so?"

"I know so, sweetie. I've seen it enough times to know. It's hard to let go, but they learn. You and Cleo make a good couple. You're good for each other. Romaine was never good for her. You will be. You love her, don't you?"

"I do, Ella, I really do."

"Good."

Romaine was drying the dishes as Cleo washed them. Romaine missed times like these, and she wished she had appreciated them while they were happening.

"Why is it that when we talk of our past we only remember the bad times, the fights, and all that?" Romaine asked.

Cleo looked at her and sighed. "Because there were more of them than the good moments."

"God, I fucked up, didn't I?" Romaine said.

Cleo felt tears well up. "I wish I could learn to hate you. It would make things so much easier. I loved you more than I've ever loved anyone, and all you did was shit on me!" Cleo said, hitting Romaine's chest with both fists and then running from the room.

"Cleo, wait!" Romaine said, running after her. But Cleo locked herself in her room. Romaine slumped outside the door. She heard Cleo crying long into the night. When the tears finally stopped, Romaine let herself out quietly and drove home. She felt worse than she had in her entire life. It was the first time the gravity of her actions had touched her, and she felt them acutely.

The next morning Romaine brought her flowers. Cleo looked at them through red eyes.

"I'm sorry. If you never want to speak to me again, I'll understand," Romaine said, sheepishly.

Cleo opened the screen door. "If only that were possible. Come in and have some coffee."

Romaine kissed her cheek. "Thank you."

Cleo poured coffee, and Romaine found a vase for the dozen white daylilies. They were Cleo's favorite.

"Why are you always sweet and thoughtful after you're such a beast? Why can't you be like this without the other part?"

"I'm schizophrenic?"

"I mean it, Romaine, why?"

"I don't know why. I do bad things and I know I'm doing them, but I can't seem to make myself stop. It's as if I have an evil twin that despises harmony. I wish someone would make me better, kill the demon. I could be good. I have moments, but then something inside me snaps. I hurt everyone I touch," Romaine said, tears building up. Cleo held her.

She wiped Romaine's eyes. "I want you to try to straighten things out with Cynthia. She loves you, and she needs you. With her you might have a chance to repair what you've done. I want you to stop thinking about us. We've had our time, and now we've got to let go. Okay?" Cleo said, looking her straight in the eye.

"All right, I'll try. Can I still come over for dinner? Her cooking will never be as good as yours."

"Yes."

"I just can't imagine my life without you in it."

"We've always been a part of each other's lives. That won't change. Maybe if we stop being lovers we can start being friends and our relationship will get better. Let's try."

"Okay. I still love you."

"I know. But no more nonsense. Promise?"

"I never thought I'd be forced to grow up in my forties. It's so tedious sometimes."

"You can't stay a wicked teenager your whole life. You begin to look rather foolish after a while. You don't want to end up like Teen Angel do you?"

"God no. He was disgusting," Romaine replied, thinking of the awful old man always out cruising younger and younger women. He was the town joke.

"It could happen."

"It won't. I'll grow up even if it kills me. Maybe being responsible and decent isn't as dull as I've always thought it would be."

"You should give it a try before you condemn it. Besides, at the rate you're going you're bound to become a statistic for a violent death perpetrated by one you love."

"Are you threatening me or planning something big? You're still my beneficiary."

"No, though I can't say I haven't thought about it. But you do seem to bring out the worst in people."

"Thanks."

"Realizing your faults is part of growing up."

"Can I go now?"

"Yes, darling."

"What are you doing?" Romaine asked as Cleo picked up a butcher knife.

"I'm going to perform an operation."

"What sort of an operation?"

"Cut out the evil twin."

"I'm leaving."

Fourteen

Romaine sat with her head in her hands. Something was happening to her that she didn't know how to stop. A crucial part of her was being amputated, sucked out, leaving her limp and frightened. Were these growing pains? Was it possible to grow up and act responsible at forty?

In the past few days she forced herself to look backward, to examine what she had done to herself and the women she slept with. In her own way she had loved them all, maybe not the same way she loved Cleo, but she wasn't as malicious as people thought.

Hers was a whimsical heart, and she had a difficult time keeping it on course. The grass was always greener over there, and she was attractive and charming. She got whatever she wanted. What she needed was for someone to say no, but none of them had. They'd gone with her willingly, knowing that they took her away from her wife, and none had cared until they too were left. *What sort of sickness is this? What awful malady does the human soul possess that creates such horrific cruelties of the heart?* Romaine asked herself.

If her mother hadn't labored for years under the ardent care of a variety of psychiatrists, Romaine might have gone into therapy, allowing an outside party to examine her foibles. But she didn't trust them. With each passing year her mother became weirder, more selfish, and more neurotic. Romaine couldn't stand to be around her. She left one day and never looked back; her mother's illness had become a pillar of salt Romaine had no taste for.

She shed her past like a worn, ugly winter coat, slashing remorse from her list of qualities with a quick flick of her wrist, living in the present with complete disregard for what had gone before.

Maybe she had whimsical genes? Her mother was an emotional chameleon; there was no anticipating her next move. She traded friends and lovers like outfits in a day.

Deep down Romaine knew where she had learned her bad behavior. *If they don't make you happy, trade them in.* Romaine had no tolerance for the occasional boredom of a long relationship, nights without passion, the everydayness of marriage. The stasis of emotion drove her to madness. She hated complaisance and sought only heights and crevasses, flying or falling, never walking on flat land.

Now in the throes of indecision she craved stasis, wanted familiar arms, needed flat land, feared heights and secret dark places. But there were no arms to hold her or hands to brush away her tears. She picked up her paintbrushes instead and painted brooding images. They made her feel better. Like a bleeding of the soul, art functioned emotionally as a pail of leeches once had done physically.

One afternoon when Cynthia came to see her, she found Romaine standing in front of her painting, holding a brush.

"Hi," Cynthia said from the open doorway.

Romaine looked at Cynthia as if she were seeing her for the first time. She had forgotten how pretty she was in her city editor jeans, boots, white shirt, and camel hair blazer. She couldn't cook, but she dressed well.

"How are you?" Romaine asked, setting her brush down.

"I've been better."

"Me too."

Cynthia walked over and looked at the painting. "Nice, very nice."

"I'm sorry I hurt you. I don't know why I do things like that. I can't stop myself from hurting people," Romaine blurted out, tears starting to fall.

Cynthia had never seen Romaine cry. In the countless arguments, the myriad screaming fights, the soothing apologies, no tears had come from Romaine. Cynthia melted. She had come to make amends, to take Romaine on whatever terms she desired. She missed Romaine. She couldn't make herself stop loving her. She came back without pride, without demands.

She took Romaine in her arms and held her. When the sobs subsided, she wiped her tears away and looked Romaine in the eyes. "I love you, and no matter how I've tried I can't make myself stop. I want to be with you, whatever that means."

Romaine looked at her. "I've missed you. I know I'm rotten, but I'll try to be better."

Cynthia kissed her softly, ardently. "I've missed you too."

She kissed Romaine's neck, undid her shirt, took her breasts in her mouth, ran her hand down her lean stomach.

Cynthia looked up at her. "Can we?"

"Please."

They went to bed. Romaine let herself go. Let herself be seduced, swallowed up in the emotion, let her lover inside. Cynthia held her, both of them shaking and sweaty. She knew something was different; Romaine felt changed to her. She was more vulnerable, less in control. Cynthia felt she had touched Romaine deep in some hidden place. She murmured her love, and Romaine kissed her. Romaine wasn't ready to say "I love you," but she was getting closer. Cynthia would wait.

Later Cynthia got up to go, and Romaine pulled her back.

"Don't go. Stay with me."

Cynthia looked at her in the shimmering light of neon darkness. She gladly stayed. Each time she woke during the night, she gazed upon her lover, praying she was strong enough to make Romaine say those words. She wanted to wake up next to her the rest of her days. But could she persuade Romaine?

In the morning she woke to a naked Romaine bringing her coffee and rolls in bed. Cynthia sat up rubbing her eyes.

"Have I died and is this heaven and are you my personal angel?" Cynthia chided.

"I'm going to try," Romaine said sheepishly. She felt vulnerable, and it scared her.

Cynthia reached for her. "I love you, and I won't hurt you."

"I don't know why I'm this way," Romaine said.

Cynthia sat up and held her. "We can do this if you want to, and I know you can. All I ask is that you try. I don't expect miracles, but I want to be more than one of your passing fancies. Someday I'd like to be your wife. It doesn't have to be tomorrow, but someday."

Romaine looked at her. Cynthia wasn't Cleo, never would be, but she was a nice woman, a kindhearted woman, and maybe they could make a go of it, start over, and Romaine would be good and commit herself to one woman and not be forever wandering and killing hearts.

"That's what I want. I'll have to learn."

"I'm a patient woman. I'll wait."

They held each other, and each believed the other. Cynthia gave her heart willingly, and Romaine took it in her tentative hands and promised to be kind.

* * * * *

Cleo smiled at them when they strolled in the restaurant for lunch.

"Now this is a welcome sight," Cleo said.

Cynthia looked at her. "You are an *incredible* woman."

"Nah, I'm hoping you can fix my botched-up job."

"Is that what I am, your botched-up job?" Romaine asked, furrowing her brow.

"I won't treat you like one when you stop acting like one," Cleo said.

"All right," Romaine said, taking Cynthia's hand.

Frankie felt herself breathing easier. If those two stayed together, she wouldn't have to worry. She kept finding herself watching Cleo for signs of wanting Romaine back. She hated herself for doing it, but she couldn't stop. She wanted to spend her energies being in love, not looking for remorse in her lover. She knew she was as much under Romaine's spell as Cleo, and they both desperately needed to break away.

Frankie smiled at them, hoping their love could save her own. Cleo took her hand and looked at her lovingly. Maybe they could break free. Maybe there was a way out. Cleo's smiling eyes seemed to whisper those words. Frankie held her close, an offering to an angry goddess.

Fifteen

Cleo was trying to make out Frankie's voice across the crackling telephone wire. A tremendous storm whipped outside. The rain was coming down in glaring sheets, and water was running everywhere. The thirsty land now saturated was unable to swallow one more drop.

"Do you want me to come get you?"

"No, I'm afraid of the roads. I'll get a hotel. They've rescheduled the concert for next week," Frankie said.

"I'll miss you. Will you come for coffee in the morning?"

"Of course. Is it pouring there too?"

"I haven't seen a storm this bad in years. I can only imagine the havoc it's creating in my gardens," Cleo fretted.

"I'll help you clean them up," Frankie offered.

"I love you," Cleo said, without thinking. They were both silent for a moment.

"I love you too."

"Come home soon, okay?"

"Early, I'll be home early."

When she got to the hotel room, Frankie pulled out the pouch with the stones Cleo had given her. She put the purple amethyst in the soft leather pouch and held it tightly in her hand. *She loves me, she loves me! Yes, me.* She fell asleep and dreamed of Cleo.

Puzzled, Cleo answered the knock at the door. Romaine stood soaking wet without a coat, her hair whipping around her face. She'd been crying.

"Romaine, what are you doing? You're soaked. Come inside," Cleo said, opening the screen door.

"I can't believe this is happening," Romaine said.

"What is happening?" Cleo said, equally mystified.

"That we're over."

"Who's over?"

"Fucking pay attention!" Romaine screamed. "Us, you and me, twenty years, over! I can't believe it." She crumbled into a ball on Cleo's wood floor, leaving puddles everywhere.

For a moment Cleo winced and thought about mentioning to Romaine that she was ruining the floor, but she decided it would be tacky in this moment of need. Instead, she knelt next to her, lifting up her face. "We're not over, we're just changing. I'll still be there whenever you need me. I promise."

Romaine stared at her through tears. "You want to get rid of me!" She began sobbing again.

"Jesus, Romaine, this is enough. You're wet. You've got to get out of those clothes or you'll catch cold. You've got to get a grip on yourself. Now come on."

Cleo marched her in the direction of the tub, ran water, and made Romaine take her clothes off.

"I'm going to get you something to drink, something to take the edge off, and then we'll talk."

"Make it a large dose of hemlock, please," Romaine said, easing her cold body down into the steamy tub.

"Stop it!"

"Yes, ma'am."

Cleo made her an Irish coffee and vied for time, trying to think. *I can't do this again. I can't let her do this to me again. One of us has to break this cycle, or it will endlessly repeat itself. It must stop.* Cleo kept seeing Frankie in her mind and thinking, *I do love her. She's not Romaine, but she is the woman I want to be with.* She took a deep breath and went to face Romaine.

Handing her the coffee, she sat down on the commode.

Romaine sipped it, purring her content.

"Are you calmed down enough to talk?"

"Yes, I feel better, thank you. I don't know what happened. I was painting, and I got to thinking about us. I realized how much I still love you and that letting you go is going to hurt."

Cleo put her head in her hands, half laughing, half sighing.

"Romaine, *you are* fucking hopeless."

"What?"

"Did it ever occur to you that every time you left me, every time you fucked someone else, that I still loved you and that letting go hurt?"

"I suppose it did," Romaine murmured, taking another sip. This conversation was not working in her favor. She wasn't entirely sure what she wanted or why she was here. She had come because she had to.

"I should have taken you out back and shot you years ago. That way you wouldn't have spent the rest of your life being a scourge to the lesbian nation."

"I resent that!"

"Sometimes you make me so mad. You're so self-centered it's pathetic," Cleo said, getting up suddenly and grabbing Romaine's ankles, yanking her entire body, head included, underwater.

Romaine came up sputtering and mad. "You tried to drown me!"

"Don't tempt me," Cleo said, handing her a towel.

Romaine yanked on the towel and pulled Cleo tottering into the tub. She landed on top of Romaine.

"Damn you, Romaine!"

"Paybacks are hell," Romaine said, smiling and grabbing Cleo.

"You're just starting to find out."

"Is that what this is about? Is Frankie a payback?"

"No, I love Frankie. Learning to hurt is the payback."

Tears filled Romaine's eyes.

"Don't start," Cleo said, holding Romaine.

Cleo kissed away her tears. "Shhh, let's get dried off. Come on."

Romaine kissed her, gently at first, until Cleo found herself succumbing, not meaning to, but wanting to. She let Romaine take her to bed.

It was a time warp. The first and last time they made love and all the times in between seemed to roll into one. They knew each other's bodies better than they knew their own, lost in what's yours and what's mine. Cleo opened her eyes to see Romaine's stomach arching and rocking across her own damp skin. She had loved this woman for such a long time. Could she let go? Could this be the last time?

It frightened her to let Romaine go, but they would end as lovers, not enemies. They would learn to become friends.

Cleo closed her eyes and let Romaine take her. She would deal with the consequences later. She knew there would be some difficult ones. But tonight, there was rain, tears, love, and Romaine in her arms.

Sixteen

Frankie poured Romaine and Cleo coffee. It was still raining, and it had taken her most of the morning to get back. She missed the breakfast shift but helped with lunch.

"I still don't think it was a good idea to travel in this weather," Cleo reprimanded her.

"I wanted to get back. Besides, the forecast is for rain through the night. I drove slowly."

"At least it was daylight and you're safe," Romaine said, being uncommonly civil to Frankie.

Frankie went to take a customer's order. Cleo

glanced at Romaine. It was odd to think she had waked next to Romaine and now the two of them were having coffee with Cleo's girlfriend. Cleo wasn't certain how to feel. She wasn't sure if making love to your ex-wife was full-fledged adultery or simply a miscalculation in judgment. She couldn't imagine how Frankie would see it.

Romaine promised never to say anything to anyone, and she had been well behaved in the morning. She said she felt better about letting go because they had said hello by making love and that saying good-bye the same way seemed a proper closure. Cleo understood her need for closure; she had had so little of it in her life. Maybe this would help. Maybe Romaine was growing up. She had promised to settle down and stop breaking hearts, and this time Cleo believed her. She had no other choice.

"I swear, Romaine, if you fuck this one up, if this is the one secret you can't keep, I will never speak to you again as long as I live. I mean that."

"I won't let you down," Romaine said, holding her tightly.

Cleo felt pangs of guilt, but finishing up with Romaine was something she'd had to do before she could truly give herself to Frankie.

The door swung open with clattering force as the bells hit the glass. Both Romaine and Cleo swiveled around to see Cynthia stomping toward them. She did not look happy. Cleo's heart leaped into her throat.

Romaine jumped up. "Darling," she said, hoping to defuse, divert, anything. She was scrambling for ground.

"Don't you *darling* me. You said you wouldn't do shit like this anymore with your ex-wife."

Frankie turned around and looked at them.

"Yeah, did you know that? Did you know what your girlfriend was doing last night? It wasn't sleeping alone."

"What are you talking about?" Romaine said, vying for time. If she could get Cynthia out of here before the whole thing blew up, she could at least save Cleo grief.

"You know damn well what I'm talking about. I was at the studio. I drove around town to all the bars and to some of your friends. Then at three in the morning I found your car parked at Cleo's house. All the lights were out, and I'm not stupid. It wouldn't take a rocket scientist to know what was going on. Are you two getting back together and just haven't had the balls to tell anyone?" Cynthia glared.

For once Romaine didn't opt for deception. Cleo didn't know if it was an improvement or a penalty for the two of them.

Frankie watched Cleo and knew the words Cynthia spoke were true. She waited for the words to bring her house of glee to its knees.

"I don't expect you to understand, but it was good-bye. We were saying good-bye," Romaine said.

"By fucking each other's brains out," Cynthia said, slapping Romaine across the face. Romaine grabbed her wrist and held her against the wall.

Cleo watched as the veins in Romaine's neck bulged.

"Don't ever say that! It wasn't like that."

"Then what was it like? Just some gentle farewell crotch rubbing?" Cynthia asked, beginning to squirm.

"Why did you come here?"

"Because I want the truth."

"What good will that do? You already figured it out."

"Why? I want to know why."

"I don't know why. It just happened, but now it's over and it won't happen again, ever."

"And you expect me, us," Cynthia said, looking over at Frankie who stood staring, "to believe that."

"Yes," Romaine said.

"Well, I won't. You can both fuck off and die so far as I'm concerned. You deserve each other."

Frankie took one look at Cleo and bolted for the door.

Romaine held Cynthia against the wall. "I love you, dammit, and if you think I'm going to let go you're crazy. I want to be with you. I want to live with you. I want us to be together. Please."

Cynthia looked at Romaine and burst into tears. She had waited, desperately wanting to hear those words, and now when she wanted to kill Romaine for hurting her, she fell into her arms willingly.

"I love you."

Alice poked Cleo.

"Do something!"

"Like what?" Cleo asked her.

"Go after her," Alice replied.

Cleo ran out into the streaming rain. She saw Frankie walking across the back fields behind the restaurant.

"Frankie, wait!" Cleo screamed into the whipping wind.

Frankie turned around. "I trusted you. How could you do this?"

"I'm sorry. I'm so sorry."

"You made me love you, and the whole time I was just a pawn to get Romaine back."

"It's not like that."

"Forget it. Go back to Romaine. Cynthia's right. You two deserve each other," Frankie said, walking off.

Cleo grabbed her, tears in her eyes. "No, I want you. I love you. Please, please don't go."

Frankie glared at her. "Don't you understand? I can't live that way, always wondering when you'll go back, wondering when you'll need a quick fix of that woman. I can't and I won't. Now let go of me!"

"No," Cleo said, hanging on tighter. They struggled and fell into the muddy field. Frankie squirmed loose.

"Leave me alone," Frankie said, leaving Cleo sitting in the mud, crying.

Cleo watched her walk off, knowing it was hopeless. She had lost the one woman who had broken Romaine's spell. *Fucking Romaine. She ruins everything she touches.* When she got cold enough, she wandered home feeling hopeless and alone.

This was like the first time she had lost Romaine. This is what you get for falling in love, she told herself as she stood in the shower trying to wash the mud, anger, and heartbreak off.

Romaine took Cynthia home, her hand upon her thigh, not wanting to lose contact with her for a moment. She ran her a hot bath and gently removed her wet clothes. She washed Cynthia's back, kissed her neck, held her, whispered "I love you" over and over again, kissed her tears away, and took her to bed. Romaine held her until she stopped crying and then slowly made love to her, trying to take the hurt away and replace it with love. She held her until she fell asleep, and she watched her for hours after that.

In the morning she awoke to Cynthia holding her and smiling. "Do you still love me this morning?" she asked weakly.

Romaine squeezed her tight. "More than you'll ever know."

Seventeen

"Alice, what am I going to do?" Cleo asked, sipping a beer.

"Hire a new waitress, for one thing."

"What do you mean?"

"It's been two days. I've talked to Ella, and she said Frankie won't come in because she's afraid she'll see you, and she can't bear that. She said it's one of the pitfalls of dating the boss. When you break up, you can't come to work."

"Alice, you're not helping the situation," Cleo moaned.

"I could call and tell her that you won't come in when she's here," Alice suggested. "She'll stay in town at least. Give you time to patch things up."

Cleo looked at her. "Oh my god, I didn't even think about her leaving. Call her. Tell her I promise... maybe that's not the most appropriate word to use."

"She doesn't exactly think you're trustworthy."

"I'm aware of that."

"Why did you two do that?"

"I don't know. Romaine was having a bad moment, and I guess I got caught up in it."

"It just figures. Romaine starts everything, still gets to keep the girl, and meanwhile back at the farm you end up alone."

"Romaine always gets what she wants."

"You aren't giving up, are you?"

"I don't know what to do."

"How about being aggressive for a change?"

"What do you mean?"

"Go talk to her."

"And say what?"

"You're sorry and you love her."

"I tried that already. She thinks I'm using her to get at Romaine."

"But surely Romaine's being with Cynthia changes all that."

"I don't think so. If it did, she'd come around."

"She's ultrapissed," Alice said, shaking her head, making her dangling orange ball earrings swing in unison. She looked like a tangerine tree in heat.

"It's beyond that. I think she always held Romaine and me suspect, and when we slipped up it confirmed her suspicions."

"But she told me she loves you."

"You can love someone, but if you can't trust her, it doesn't work."

"So you guys are finished, kaput?"

"Before we really got started."

"Did you sleep together?"

"Alice!"

"Did you?" Alice said, totally undaunted by Cleo's hint at discretion.

"Well, no."

"You guys are pathetic. If you had, I guarantee she wouldn't be walking away so easily."

"That's sick."

"No, it's not. You exchange something when you make love, and it's not an easy thing to walk away from. You've been vulnerable with another person. And no matter how mad you are at her, in the back of your mind you still remember how it felt holding her wet and sweaty in your arms, her legs wrapped around your face..."

"Alice, that's enough."

"I'm sorry. Sometimes I just get lost in the beauty of the whole thing. Anyway, the point I was trying to make was, what did you leave her with, a few good times, some laughs, but nothing permanent?"

"You're saying if I put my hand in her crotch she'd be mine."

"Talk about my graphic descriptions, what was that about?"

"I'm frustrated."

"If you weren't such a prude with your girlfriend and such a slut with your wife, you wouldn't be having this problem."

"I know. Will you call her?"

"Yes, if you promise you won't give up."

"I won't. Not yet."

Cleo went home and sat in her rocker on the porch to think. She hadn't felt so discombobulated since the first time Romaine wandered off.

Is this how Romaine felt when she realized she'd made a grave mistake in straying? Had she ever worried she might not be able to go back? What if I hadn't wanted her back? What if she had fallen in love with someone else? Is this how it feels to lose the one you should have spent your life with? Always pining for the lost one, knowing the fuck-up had been crucial, spending the rest of your life with a substitute for the one you really want?

Cleo still didn't understand how it had happened. It had been a momentary lapse. But could she be trusted not to do it again? Maybe Frankie was right in thinking that she would never be able to let go of Romaine.

Was my making love with Romaine really a secret solemn promise that it would never be over? A spell, a curse, a mistake endlessly repeated? Can I give Romaine up? Maybe it's better to let Frankie go. I can't ask Frankie to live in the shadow of a perverted lifelong romance. Cleo looked up to see her nemesis rolling up in the driveway.

"How are you?" Romaine smiled, kissing her cheek.

"Not great."

"So I heard."

"Alice?"

"Who else but a bad drag queen. I'm sorry. I didn't think they'd find out. Not that that makes it right. I guess we're hard to figure. I stopped by to see if there was anything I could do to, you know, make amends."

"I think it's past that. I fucked up, and it appears there's no going back. Live with the consequences and all that."

Eighteen

Frankie lay on her bed, her hands behind her head, counting the ceiling tiles. She'd been doing this for several days. Ella had been up to talk to her numerous times. Frankie responded in monosyllables.
 She should leave. There wasn't any reason to stay. She had been staying because she was in love. Now she didn't know. Go back. *Go back to what? Electra and her group of fucked-up friends? Go back to stare out at the sea and dream of Cleo?*
 Go back to work and try to avoid Cleo? Ella told her that Alice had called and said that Cleo promised

to stay clear. It would be easy enough to do. But the restaurant reminded her of Cleo, so what was it really achieving? She missed Cleo. She loved Cleo. She hurt. Would leaving put an end to the pain? She didn't know. She stared at the ceiling and prayed for a miracle.

It was night when Cleo wandered into the restaurant. Frankie's bike was nowhere to be seen. She was fugitive now, in her own life, in her business, in her heart. Alice was dressed in a purple miniskirt and white frilly blouse. Cleo looked down at her own ensemble, a pair of olive-green overall shorts and an undershirt. *Maybe it's the way I dress. I can't keep a girlfriend because I'm not spiffy enough,* she thought to herself. She laughed out loud. *No, it's because I'm psychotic.*

"Are you laughing at my outfit again?" Alice said, swiveling around.

"No, I wasn't. I swear. Jo, can you get me a beer and a tequila?"

"Hitting the hard stuff?" Alice asked, raising an eyebrow.

"I need to get some sleep. It's hard with insomnia."

"Guilty conscience?"

Cleo looked at her strangely. "Should I have one?"

Alice cocked her head. "I don't rightly know. Romaine is or was your wife; you hadn't made any kind of commitment to Frankie; I guess there are certain technicalities."

"Is she pissed?"

"Frankie?"

"Yeah."

"She's quiet, pale, and thinner. All signs of depression, I'd say."

"Does she hate me?"

"I don't know. She's not talking."

"Oh, Alice," Cleo said, sinking down at the bar. "Jo, another tequila shot."

"Honey, if you're going to drink, why don't you come out to the bar with me and we'll do it up proper. I'll drive you home, and I guarantee you'll sleep like a baby. Jo, make me one too, the girls are going out partying," Alice said, doing a neat little shuffle.

"I don't think so," Cleo said.

"You haven't got any choice. Now drink up."

Cleo found herself sitting at the bar of the Nip and Tuck. She quickly surveyed the sisters while they gave her the once-over. She saw a couple of quick nudges, so she knew her indiscretion was all over town again. Theresa and Faye came over and gave their condolences.

"It's not like there's been a death in the family," Alice said, perturbed. She had brought Cleo here to take her mind off it, not to be reminded she had a psychotic attachment to her ex-wife.

"It's just too bad. I had such high hopes for Cleo. I really thought she could make a go of it with someone other than Romaine," Theresa said, flicking her long blond hair over her shoulder.

Cleo signaled to the bartender for another beer.

"Not a word out of you, Madge," Cleo said.

"Who I am to say? We all fuck up. Lord knows I've done it enough times. Maybe Frankie will get over it and you guys can kiss and make up. Stranger things have happened. Speak of the devil," Madge said, looking in the direction of the door.

"What?" Cleo asked without turning around.

"It's Frankie and Ella. Must be everyone's night out."

Cleo glared at Alice. "You planned this, didn't you?"

"No, I swear. Ella probably thought Frankie needed some diversion."

"Where's she going?" Cleo asked.

"You can turn around. It's not against the law."

"I can't look at her. Alice, we've got to get out of here."

"Why don't you guys talk?"

"Talk about what? She doesn't trust me. I broke her heart, and that's it, end of story."

"She might be willing to change her mind with the right kind of persuasion."

"What kind of persuasion?"

"Use your imagination."

Cleo ordered another beer and tried to think. All she could think of was how to escape without being seen. She felt someone sit down beside her. She looked over. It was Frankie.

"Hi," Frankie said.

Cleo fell into her eyes, wishing she could fall into her arms, make love, and forget everything.

"Hi, how are you?"

"Not great. And yourself?"

Cleo looked straight ahead at the bar. "Awful, I'm just awful."

"You're right. You are awful, but I miss you.

Look, you don't have to avoid me at work. I thought about it, and it's stupid. It is your restaurant, and I'm a big girl."

"Okay," Cleo said, trying hard not to cry. "Look, I'm really sorry about all that."

"I know. It just happened, and now it's over. We made good friends. We shouldn't have to forfeit that, should we?" Frankie said tentatively. She didn't know how to suggest they simply forget it and start over.

Cleo looked at her as if Frankie had punched her. She burst into tears and ran out of the bar.

Frankie ran after her. "Cleo, wait!"

Frankie caught her in the parking lot. She grabbed her arm, stopping her.

Cleo was drunk, lost, and hurting. Frankie pulled her in close, and their bodies got a quick fix, feeling each other again. Cleo sobbed, and Frankie held her.

"Shhh, now come on. I thought it would make you feel better. I want to see you again," Frankie said.

Cleo pulled away. "I don't want to be your friend. I want to be your lover. I can't be friends. I love you. I can't stop touching you or wanting you. I want us to be together. This is why I never wanted to fall in love. People always leave. I love them, and they leave. I can't fucking believe it. I let myself love you, and now this... I know it's my fault, and if I could make it go away I would, I swear. I can't!" Cleo screamed, then ran off, leaving Frankie standing there speechless.

Frankie meant to get her back, not send her packing. She had hoped if they could be friends they could start over and ease into being lovers. She thought she was taking a crucial first step putting fear aside, but now it seemed she'd botched the thing. She didn't know how else to do it. She stood there looking up at the night sky, still wishing for a miracle or at least the right prayer.

"What did you say to her?" Alice asked.

Frankie turned around. "I botched it. I wanted to see if we could make amends. I told her I wanted us to be friends, and she got upset."

"Jesus, you two are the worst lesbians I've ever known. Christ, are you mad!"

"What?"

"You never tell someone you want to sleep with that you want to be friends. Do you want to be lovers?"

"Yes, very much."

"Then why say *friend* when you mean more?"

"I don't know," Frankie stuttered. "Oh, Alice!" and she burst out in tears.

"Come here, honey, ah come on. We'll get it all fixed up, okay?"

Nineteen

Romaine strolled into the restaurant, and Frankie made an instant beeline for the kitchen. Romaine appeared preoccupied and didn't seem to notice. Alice did.

"Alice have you seen Cleo lately? I've been by the house several times, and she's never home. Did those two," Romaine said, cocking her head in the direction of the kitchen, "you know, make up and they're shacking up somewhere?"

"I don't know where she is. It seems that Frankie tried to talk to her, see if they could patch things up, but Cleo ran off."

"Has anyone seen her?"

"Not that I know of. Not here at least. She's probably taking a few days off."

"That's fine, but where is she?"

"Are you sure she's just not answering the door?"

"I have a key. I used to live there, remember? I checked. She's not there."

"You should have stayed living there, and then there wouldn't be this mess," Alice said under her breath.

"I heard that. Life's not that simple, and neither are my habits. This is my fault; I understand that, and if I could make it go away I would. If you see her, call me."

Romaine went around to all the bars, their friends, every place she could think of. By the end of the day she was really worried. The odd thing was the truck. Cleo's truck was still parked in the driveway. Did she take a bus somewhere? Romaine went to the bus station. Nothing there. Finally she went home with a growing sick feeling in her stomach.

"Romaine, what's wrong?" Cynthia asked when she got home. Romaine was halfway through a pitcher of martinis. Cynthia knew that she was stress drinker. And Cynthia knew that when it was serious Romaine drank martinis.

"Cleo's missing."

"What do you mean?"

"We can't find her anywhere. She didn't take her truck or the bus out of town. God, if anything's happened to her it's all my fault."

Cynthia came over and gave her a hug. "We'll find her."

Romaine looked at her gratefully and took her hand. "I don't know what I'd do without you. I put you through hell, and you still love me."

"Of course, and since I love you so much I'll cut your tits off if you go off and leave me for another woman, Cleo included."

"I won't. Believe me I'm done with that."

Bobbi McCormick answered the door. It was Cleo. She was dirty, dripping with sweat, and tired.

"Cleo, what are you doing here?"

"I needed a refuge."

"Sweetheart, come in. Where's the truck?" Bobbi asked, looking out into the empty drive.

"It's at home," Cleo said, taking her boots off.

"How did you get here?"

"I walked."

"You walked."

"Yep. Had some thinking to do."

"How long did that take?"

"About three days," Cleo said matter-of-factly.

"You walked for three days?"

"Yep. Do you have a beer?"

"Yes, of course. So let me get this straight. You walked here."

"Over the pass and through the hills and down Miller's Crossing. Now, do you think I could have that beer? Why don't people walk places anymore?" Cleo said, getting mildly perturbed at the twenty-question quiz.

"Darling, it's fifty miles."

"I'm aware of that. I just started walking and thinking and I needed someone to talk to, so I thought I'd come see you."

"What did she do now?" Bobbi asked, getting herself a glass of wine and sitting down.

"She's mad at me because I let her down by sleeping with Romaine one last time, accidentally."

"How do you sleep with someone accidentally?"

"Kind of like we almost accidentally slept together."

"It wasn't accidental on my part," Bobbi said, smiling and taking Cleo's hand. "I've missed you."

"I've missed you too. I wish you'd come back. Aren't you through being angry with us?"

"I'm almost there. I was thinking about coming down for a visit. Now wait a minute. Who is *she*?"

"What do you mean?"

"The *she* who's mad at you for accidentally sleeping with Romaine."

"Frankie."

"You mean to tell me that you finally slept with someone other than Romaine? You beast. I wanted that honor," Bobbi said, picking up the nearest pillow and hitting Cleo with it repeatedly.

"We haven't slept together," Cleo cried out.

"You're not lovers?"

"We were working in that direction until the accident."

"Oh, I get it now. She doesn't trust you."

"Exactly. She thought that maybe I was using her

to get back at Romaine, and when Romaine and I slept together, that's what it looked like. But Cynthia and Romaine are living together. They managed to patch it up."

"It figures that you're the one left out in the cold."

"Pretty much. The other night Frankie and I talked at the bar, and she said she wanted to be friends. I don't want to be friends. I can't be like that now. I want to be lovers."

"Oh my, karma comes to visit. Now you know what it feels like."

"I know. I'm sorry. But being lovers does ruin things. If Frankie and I hadn't gotten romantic, we'd still be friends. Now everything's fucked up."

"What do you propose to do?"

"Stay away. Maybe then she'll move on, and I can start to forget," Cleo said, looking down at her hands. It was the best she could come up with. With time they'd both forget. Frankie would find someone else, and Cleo figured she'd move gracefully into old age alone. Love obviously wasn't her forte.

During the delirium of her walk, Cleo had kept playing scenes from her life with Romaine and then her life with Frankie until everything jostled together. The two women fused to become some monstrous vision of tormented love. All squeezed and twisted, the good things about love were no longer visible. What Cleo hated most was hurting Frankie the same way Romaine had always hurt her, as if the cycle couldn't be broken. Cleo had become another version of Romaine, making women fall in love with her only to torment them by committing infidelities.

"Cleo! How can you say that!" Bobbi interjected, snapping Cleo back from her wandering.

"Very easily, you just go like this with your lips," Cleo said, moving her lips mouthing the words.

Bobbi came over and beat her silly with the pillow until she screamed out for mercy. Bobbi kissed her cheek.

"No offense Cleo, but you stink," Bobbi said, getting off her and pushing her in the direction of the bathroom.

Cynthia was making coffee when the thought struck her. "Romaine, have you tried Bobbi's? Maybe she went there."

Romaine grabbed her Rolodex. "God, I bet you're right."

"What, didn't she leave a note?" Bobbi asked when Romaine had her on the line.

"Bobbi, come on. Can't we let bygones be bygones?" Romaine asked.

"It's not your heart we're talking about. Besides it's not me I'm concerned with. I can't believe after all this time that you're still fucking up Cleo's life."

"So she's there?"

"Yes, she's sleeping right now."

"How is she?"

"She's okay, considering how she got here. Tired and hungry."

"Did you come pick her up?"

"No, she walked here."

"Oh my."

"I'd say she was pretty distraught, wouldn't you?"

"Can I come get her?"

"No."

"Why not?" Romaine asked, exasperated.

"Romaine, why is it that when you live with her you treat her like shit, and when you're away you behave decently, almost with a certain tenderness? Why is that?"

"Because I'm psychotic. I don't know. I'm trying to improve, believe it or not."

"I don't. You fucked up her one chance at happiness. She's given up on Frankie, and I know she won't try again. This is on you, Romaine. It's your fault. So don't tell me you're changing. I'll bring her home when she's ready."

Romaine slammed the receiver down. Cynthia looked up from her proofs.

"Fucking bitch!" Romaine said. She hated when other people were right. When was she going to stop fucking up Cleo's life? It wasn't like she could go talk to Frankie, who wouldn't speak to her anyway, and say, Do you think you could go get Cleo, fall madly in love, and take care of her the rest of your days so I don't have to feel guilty for mucking things up. All this chaos over one last roll in the hay. Why were people such sticklers for details?

It was a minor indiscretion and they'd been doing it their whole lives. Why should it make such a difference now? When she thought about it though, casually sleeping together had been the usual beginning to getting back together. It would happen once and then Romaine would start to crave Cleo again, like any addict, and it would start happening more frequently until whoever Romaine was dating figured it out.

"Is she there?" Cynthia asked.

"Yes."

"How is she?"

"She's not coming back for a while."

"What about Frankie?"

"She'll probably give up and leave town, and it's all my fault," Romaine said, holding her head.

"This is not good," Cynthia said, coming over and taking Romaine's hand.

Romaine looked up. "Will you promise me one thing?"

"What?"

"If I ever leave you, shoot me so I can't hurt another living being."

"Do you remember that Agatha Christie novel *Murder on the Orient Express*?"

"Yes."

"I think that's what we'll do. Maybe Frankie will stay around for a while. We'll figure something out."

"God, I hope you're right."

Twenty

"Earth calling Frankie," Alice said.

Frankie was staring out the window. She wished she could talk to Cleo, make things better. She should have been more like Cynthia and forgiven the transgression, figured it as part of their bizarre relationship. She didn't want to lose Cleo, but she felt that with each passing moment she was getting farther and farther away.

"Frankie, when you come back around would you do me a favor?"

"Huh? Oh I'm sorry, Alice. What?"

"Could you go out and pick some veggies? We seem to have lost our gardener."

"Sure," Frankie said, still preoccupied.

She got the wheelbarrow going and went about picking things. The garden was dry and parched looking; leaves were drooping everywhere. It wasn't until she picked up a squash and it fell apart in her hands, leaving her standing with rotten squash guts everywhere, that it hit her. The garden was dying. Cleo loved her plants, and she was letting them die. This was awful, and Frankie was as much to blame as Romaine for hurting her. Frankie burst into tears. She couldn't bear it. Frankie ran from the garden to her motorcycle and roared out of town.

Alice saw her go. "Christ, what now!"

Romaine strolled in looking confused. "Where's she going in such a hurry?"

"Who knows? Since Cleo's disappeared, I need help, so I sent her out to pick some produce. Then all of a sudden she charges off," Alice said, putting her hands on her hips, pursing her fuchsia lips and glaring at Romaine.

Curious, Romaine went out back to look at the garden. Alice followed her.

"What happened?" Romaine asked. "It looks like shit."

"Cleo's not been here to take care of it."

"Someone should water it at least."

"Listen, I've got a restaurant to run. My gardener's gone off, and now I've lost the wait staff. It seems to me that you're the responsible party. You started all this. You fix it," Alice said, tromping back to the kitchen.

Romaine watched her go. *She's right,* Romaine

thought. She picked up the hose and set about watering the garden. Strange, she had never set foot in the garden before. It was always Cleo's domain. Romaine had only watched her drawing up plans each season, carefully calculating germination, seedlings, present and future growth, spending hours of toil, getting tanned and strong, doing something intrinsically vital to the restaurant. Romaine had hardly given it a thought. *I really am a selfish and self-centered woman.*

She was filthy and tired when she got home. And sad, terribly sad, because she knew she squandered too many things, and there was no going back. There was no undoing all the hurt.

Cynthia ran her a bath and tried to make the pain in her lover's eyes lessen. But she, too, knew that Romaine's suffering was the only way she would get better, be better. Without it she would continue to wreck lives, her own included.

The sun was just rising across the water as Frankie sat on the shore. She always had gone there when her life was starting to suck. She went there every day when she was losing Electra, and that love affair seemed minuscule compared to this one. Frankie had never hurt so much in her whole life as she did now. She felt as if she were ready to crack open and leave little pieces of herself all over. When it was done, she'd spend the rest of her life trying to gather them up again. She didn't know what to do. She sat there listening to waves crash against the shore.

Finally tired and hungry, she went in search of food and a place to stay. It seemed strange to be back in San Francisco. She wasn't sure how she ended up here. She had kept riding, and then she remembered the ocean. She had to go see it.

She went to R and J's Coffee Shack. Frankie was reading the paper and having breakfast when she spotted her own nemesis. Women and restaurants. She was going to have to steer clear of both of them. Frankie slithered down in her chair, hoping to get out without being noticed. Electra was the one person on the entire planet she did not want to see. Frankie got up quietly and walked toward the cash register.

From across the room she heard, "Isn't that your old girlfriend?"

Electra turned around. "Frankie! How are you?"

Frankie took a deep breath and cursed herself for being so stupid. Electra loved this dive and frequented it. Frankie should have known better than to come here.

"You look like shit, darling. What's wrong? Where have you been keeping yourself?" Electra asked.

"Out of town. I just got in this morning," Frankie replied, looking at Electra and wondering how it was that she had ever fallen in love with such a woman. *Garish* came to mind. Electra had dyed her hair red and wore a considerable amount of makeup. She was pretty, but she seemed far from what Frankie viewed as desirable. Of course, now she found only one woman desirable.

"Where are you staying?" Electra asked, twirling her around and taking a good look at her.

Frankie squirmed under the inspection.

"I haven't decided yet."

"It's decided then. You can stay with Cecil and me. We're over on Fidelity Lane, number four."

"Is Cecil your girlfriend?"

"Oh no, honey. I only date."

"That's right. No home-on-the-range scene."

"You got it, darling. You still look good," Electra said, making her eyebrows quiver.

Frankie smiled weakly.

"Here, why don't you take the key, go have a nap and a bath, and we'll hook up this afternoon. It'll do you good."

"Electra, I don't think it's a good idea," Frankie replied, thinking it horrid to be revisiting circles she was trying desperately to break free from. Suddenly she felt like she was inside a Slinky.

"You don't have a choice. It's the least I can do after *all* we've been through." She thrust the key at Frankie and made ready to pout if she didn't take it.

Frankie took the key. She rode across town, thankful it was a sunny day. It was harder to be depressed. *Women. They're perfectly awful. They get you to do anything. Must we all end up with people we once slept with? Can we ever break free from the past? Or is life just one endless snare after another? Next I'll be friends with Romaine, having dinner on Saturday nights, playing golf Sunday mornings. It's sick, yet we crave it. It's why you're here, isn't it? You had an entire country to roam, and you came here.*

She climbed the four flights of stairs to the alcove apartment in an old Victorian house painted lavender, of all colors. The apartment was relatively neat for Electra. *Must be the roommate,* Frankie thought, knowing Electra was a pig. Frankie took off her clothes and showered.

When she came out wrapped in a towel, she discovered she was not alone. She stood in the middle of the floor, dripping slightly, to meet the roommate, Cecil.

"Hi, I thought it was Electra. I'm Cecil," the young blond woman said, extending her hand.

"I'm Frankie. I'm a friend of Electra's."

"More like ex-wife."

"Well, yeah."

"So are you guys hooking up again or what?"

"Oh, no," Frankie said, with such conviction that they both laughed nervously.

"She did ya in, huh," Cecil said, cracking open a beer and propping her feet up on the coffee table.

"To say the least. I know we just met, but would you happen to have a T-shirt I could borrow? I came on short notice."

"Sure. Let me get you one," Cecil said. She returned with a black Pride T-shirt.

Frankie finished dressing, feeling more human now that she was fed and clean. Amazing things, those basic necessities.

"You want a beer?" Cecil asked.

"Please," Frankie said.

"So where'd ya come from?"

"Southern Utah."

"What the hell were you doing there?"

"Visiting my aunt."

"Are you back to stay?" Cecil asked, handing her a beer.

"I don't know."

"God, you're as bad as that whimsical roommate of mine."

"I'm not even close, believe me."

Cecil chuckled. "You're probably right."

"I am."

"So you got a girlfriend?"

Frankie swallowed hard. "Not anymore."

"I'm sorry. Didn't mean to bring up a sensitive subject."

"It's okay. I'm working on it. I'll survive," Frankie said, knowing she was lying. It helped being away. In Moroni, the whole town reminded her of Cleo. Here all she saw was the city with an occasional glimpse of Electra, which she skated past with ease. Electra had simply evaporated from her mind and her heart the day she met Cleo. Love, the goddess of mutability. Plug a new love in, and the pain of the old love went away. She knew that Cleo wouldn't be easy to forget, but one can survive lost love. Cleo had been doing it forever. But Cleo always knew Romaine was coming back. It wasn't the same for Cleo and Frankie.

Frankie took a deep breath. New places, new faces were not going to give respite from the maze of emotions where she stumbled blindly, getting nowhere, tripping and kicking her own heart like an endless game of kick the can.

"Yeah, I've been there a time or two. It's funny how you feel like you're gonna die and then one day you start to feel better. You realize you're healing, and then you move on," Cecil said, looking at Frankie sideways, trying to measure the effect of her words.

Their eyes met for a moment, and Frankie noticed how blue Cecil's were, and Cecil fell into Frankie's.

"You know, I don't know who dropped you in my living room, but it was an awfully nice present," Cecil said. "Say, you want to go for a walk on the beach and grab a cone on the pier?"

Frankie blushed for a moment. "Sure."

They walked along the beach and talked. Cecil wanted to know everything about Frankie. She told most things, but she didn't talk about Cleo. It was too fresh. But she told her about Electra and why she had gone away. She told her about her music and where she hoped it would go. Cecil confessed all her past transgressions, and together they laughed about how mucked-up things get. They built a gigantic sand castle and then went for drinks at the Pink Flamingo.

It was Friday night, and the place was packed. Cecil bought her a beer, and they gawked at all the girlies. Cecil explained her rating system.

"How come nobody's snatched you up yet?" Frankie asked.

" 'Cause I'm hard to catch," Cecil said, winking at her.

"No, really."

"I just don't pick the right ones, I guess. Either they're ready to get married and we just met, or they dodge commitment like it was some kind of terrible disease, or they're psychotic. I've been kinda sticking to myself lately trying to recoup. I like to look. It's the touching that gets you in trouble."

The DJ kicked on a good song, and Cecil grabbed

Frankie. "Come on, girlie, let's go dance. Best way I know to exorcise those demons. We'll get ya cleaned out."

"You make it sound like an enema," Frankie said, getting up.

"Whatever it takes, darling," Cecil said, grabbing her hand and moving her in the direction of the dance floor.

They spent the night dancing. Every song was a good one, or so it seemed. They only stopped long enough to chug beers. The dance floor was packed, and when the music really got going and the song was right, women began taking off their shirts to reveal bras of all assortments. It was a bar perk. Cecil grabbed Frankie's T-shirt and pulled it off. They kept dancing cooler and free. Frankie had forgotten how wild the city could be. She got caught up in the dancing, drinking, and the half-naked women around her.

As they shuffled out sweaty and smiling at closing time, Cecil looked over at her and asked, "What's next?"

Frankie surprised them both by answering, "I want to go to bed ... with you."

Cecil smiled. She had wanted to touch Frankie all night. Dancing was the closest she got, but when they swung and twirled around each other, Cecil knew there was more than friendship flashing between them.

Instead of answering, she took Frankie's face in her hands and kissed her.

"I've been wanting to do that all night," she said, taking Frankie's hand and leading her in the direction of the apartment.

They kissed at every street corner, walking faster until it seemed they would never get there. Cecil undressed Frankie in the middle of the living room, ran a bath, lit candles everywhere, and thanked her lucky stars that Electra wasn't there. In the tub Cecil washed Frankie's hair, caressing her body with soap. Frankie lay against Cecil's chest while she ran her hand down Frankie's taut stomach, reaching deeper. Frankie thought she would come right there, but Cecil whispered, "Wait," and lifted her from the tub.

They wrapped themselves in towels, and Cecil led them to the bedroom. Frankie quivered with delight, aching to be touched, to be made love to until she couldn't think anymore, wouldn't hurt anymore.

Cecil eased her back onto the bed and parted her legs, taking Frankie in her mouth, entering her slowly, then more quickly, until Frankie cried out and reached for Cecil, bringing her down and feeling her deep down, drowning in the flesh of her nighttime lover. They took each other again and again from every conceivable angle, one top, one bottom, not knowing who was who until finally satiated they fell into a deep sleep.

Cecil woke up in the middle of the night, still finding herself wrapped around Frankie. She stroked Frankie's hair from her face. *I wish you were mine. But I know you're not. Whoever holds your heart was a fool to ever let you go. Love at first bite and I am smitten. Alas for an evening liaison.* Cecil smiled, pulled Frankie in tighter, and fell back asleep. *Some is better than none.*

Twenty-one

It was midmorning when Frankie awoke, looked over at Cecil, and let the memories of last night wash slowly over her. She felt better and then instantly worse. Alice was right. She and Cleo had been too careful, and because of that they lost each other. In being cautious not to want too much too quickly, they put their love on hold waiting for Romaine's next move.

Their making love had been inevitable, and it was as much Frankie's fault as it was Cleo's. Frankie sat up in bed, realizing for the first time she was losing the love of her life without ever having known it.

She slipped out of bed and found her clothes. She looked remorsefully at Cecil. She deserved better than this. Frankie hoped she would find the love she needed. Guilty, she left the house, thinking only a thief leaves without saying good-bye. Cecil would be gracious, but Frankie knew she couldn't afford to stay. She crept away, hoping Cecil would know where and why she had gone.

When Electra came home expecting to find Frankie, she was disappointed. Instead, she found Cecil still in bed, arms behind her head, smoking a cigarette and smiling.

"What pair of cat's pajamas did you eat?" Electra asked, sitting down on the edge of the bed and reaching for Cecil's cigarettes. She crossed her legs, lit a cigarette, and took a long drag. "What little darling did you stun with your loving ways?"

"What makes you think that?" Cecil said.

"Because, darling, you only look like this after you've been thoroughly fucked. Now tell."

"If you must know, it was your ex-wife."

"Frankie?"

"I believe she's the only one you have."

"Where is she?"

"Alas, my angel has flown the coop already, but it was heavenly while it lasted. Electra, you were a fool to let her go. She's in love with someone, in love and trouble. I wish it wasn't so, because I'd take her in my arms and never let her go. Still..." Cecil said, taking a drag and exhaling slowly, savoring the thought.

"But for the memory," Electra said, wrapping her gauze train around her arm and sauntering from the room with a theatrical flourish.

Cecil snuggled back beneath the covers wishing those beautiful blue eyes were still looking at her.

Alice was wiping off the last few tables from the lunch rush when Cleo came in. Romaine had just left. She was helping out at the restaurant trying to make amends for scaring off most of the help.

"Well, look who's back. Is it a special occasion?"

"I'm sorry, Alice," Cleo said, lowering her eyes like a truant schoolgirl. "I don't know what I'd do without you."

"I wish you'd tell me when you're going to go off so I could make arrangements. Romaine's been helping out. Shocking, isn't it? It seems remorse motivates her, for now, at least."

"Is she gone?"

"Romaine?"

"No, Frankie."

"Yes. It seems she ran off shortly after you did. No one's seen hide or hair of her since. Ella's a little concerned."

"Frankie's a big girl. She'll be all right. It's probably best for both of us," Cleo said, pulling a sparkling water from the bar.

"Cleo, how can you say that? You two love each other. Don't let it go like that. For once fight for someone."

"And I loved Romaine and Bobbi loved me and we all let go. This time is no different. I don't have the strength to fight anymore. If we were meant to be, none of this would have happened. End of story. Now I don't want to talk about it anymore. All right?"

Alice shook her head. "You're a fool, Cleo."

"Then I'm a fool," Cleo said, heading out the back toward the garden.

She took the wheelbarrow and set about clearing out the dead plants and weeds. Soon the garden would be back to its old self. Cleo hoped she would too. Time the healer, the most wicked and wondrous of creatures. She'd done it before; she could do it again. One day, she thought as she overturned the thick, black dirt, she would stop hurting, start to forget, and then begin to fill her life with herself again, reclaim what she had given away. She swore to herself she would never let it happen again. Cleo never hurt Cleo. It was the others, the ones she let close. But this was the last time. Not even Romaine would get through.

It was well after dark when she got home. She apologized to Marlowe the cat. Romaine had obviously been feeding her. Romaine did have her good points. She'd always been there when Cleo felt the world was closing in on her. Romaine took care of her. She didn't make a good wife, but she was a steadfast friend.

"What do I do to make them leave?" Cleo asked the night sky. "I loved them both, but I couldn't keep either one." She wrapped her arms around herself and cried, letting the night be the only witness to her pain. By morning she would put her placid face back on and walk through the rest of her life with herself as sole companion. She was the only one she could trust with her heart. Everyone else was a demon thief waiting to steal her precious organ, flaying and roasting it, making a snack of something that should have been a banquet.

She watched the moon and the stars burst forth and wondered what in the human makeup creates the need for companionship. Most of the time in a relationship is spent being bothered, upset, and fretful about a companion's lack of this or that. Nothing is ever settled. Love is an endless disappointment. Patterns persist, and so does the desire to find the perfect, ever elusive mate. We are forever thwarted in our search, yet we can't stop it. We have an autism of the heart and are unable to rid ourselves of the fixation. To be whole is to have someone love you, the biggest lie the human race has ever told itself. *For all your intellectualizing, you are still a fool,* Cleo told herself, picking up the cat and going into bed.

"I have shared my bed with you longer than any woman," Cleo told Marlowe, who settled down in the middle of the comforter, happy to have her home.

Cleo was having breakfast when she heard the distinct click of Romaine's boots on the wood floor of the restaurant. She swiveled around.

"Good morning," Cleo said.

"You could have called," Romaine said, getting herself a cup of coffee.

"Enough already. First Alice and now you. I

know, I know, I know. I promise to behave better in the future, " Cleo said, smiling at Romaine.

Romaine wrapped her arms around her and whispered in her ear, "If you ever scare me like that again, I'll never forgive you. And believe me, I'll come up with an awful punishment. Is that understood?"

"Yes, and I'm sorry."

"I missed you and I'm glad you're back and I'm sorry too," Romaine said, kissing her cheek and letting her go.

"I hear you've been helping out while I was away. I'm impressed," Cleo said.

"I don't know why you guys are so surprised. I used to help out all the time," Romaine said, knitting her eyebrows and obviously perturbed. All the commentary on her good behavior made her wonder where she'd been and what she'd been doing to make her behave so badly. *I must have been a real shit. Funny, I never noticed it before,* she thought.

"*Used to* are the key words," Alice said, trotting off to take Floyd and Charlene Perkins's order.

"That was before you got bored with it. You used to get bored real easy," Cleo chided.

"I'm working on it. Some of us are late bloomers."

"Forty-two is pushing the limits of puberty. This should have happened a long time ago," Cleo said, thinking if it had she wouldn't be hurting like this and another sweet woman would have been spared.

"It's that hindsight thing, a wonderful reminder but a relatively useless commodity," Romaine said.

"You and your commodities. Thanks for feeding Marlowe," Cleo said, taking Romaine's hand.

"Cleo, if there's anything I can do to, you know, fix things, I would," Romaine said, furrowing her brow and looking worried.

"I know."

Twenty-two

Romaine was painting and Cynthia was editing at her desk when they looked up to see Frankie standing in the doorway looking tired and dirty from the road.

"I just want to ask you one question," Frankie said.

Cynthia gathered up some papers. "I've got some things to fax," she said, leaving the room to go downstairs to the gallery.

Romaine grabbed a rag and started to clean her brush.

"What do you want to know?"

"Is it over? Is it really over?"

"It's really over," Romaine said, setting the paintbrush down and looking at Frankie.

"And how do you know that for sure?"

"That's two questions," Romaine responded. "Come in and let's have a beer. You look dry."

Frankie hesitated for a moment.

"You want an answer, don't you?"

Frankie nodded.

Romaine pulled two beers from the fridge and led them out onto the deck that overlooked the town. She handed Frankie a beer and then looked out over the buildings to the red cliffs beyond. Her eyes followed a white kite in the distance as it bobbed and twisted in the wind. Frankie followed her gaze. Romaine smiled, thinking of Cleo in her backfield, the wizard with her kite playing in the wind. Cleo was a master with a kite. Romaine had always admired her diligence, the time it took to learn the finesse of handling cloth and string against the will of nature, harnessing the wind to the point of dance, a ballet of wills producing swirls and dips of gentle motion.

Romaine turned to Frankie. "It's over because Cleo loves you. It's never been over before because Cleo never loved anyone but me. I could go back then. I can't now. And Cleo's right. It's time we stopped doing this to ourselves and to the women caught between us. Frankie, believe it or not, I want you to be with Cleo. I want you to make her happy. And I think you can."

"You didn't always think that," Frankie said.

"No, but as you now know, she's not an easy

woman to let go. I've known her most of my life. I've spent almost every day with her for half my life. It's hard."

"Then why did you let her go?"

"That's three questions," Romaine said. She let out a deep sigh. "I don't know why. I never did know why. Maybe I was afraid that if I stayed she'd be the one to leave, that if I gave everything I'd have nothing and that being empty would make me weak. I could never allow myself to be vulnerable, so I made Cleo be the one. But as time went on, she became as strong as I was, and it took more to hurt her then."

"So you slept with other women in her bed and that made it better," Frankie said, feeling vicious, wanting Romaine to hurt as she was hurting, as Cleo was hurting.

Romaine looked away, watching the kite. It was getting higher and higher.

"Yes, I suppose so. I don't expect you to understand my psychosis, but I'm the one that lives with its consequences. I lost her, but you're letting her go. Which one of us is worse? I hurt her, but you're hurting her now."

"I slept with someone else," Frankie blurted, needing to absolve herself.

Romaine chuckled. "It happens. Psychological paybacks, maybe. I wouldn't worry about it."

"I feel bad."

"Don't. You're even now."

"Is that what it's about... being even?"

"You tell me. It seems that's what we're always doing, getting even."

"Do I tell Cleo?"

"No, she doesn't need to know. It's not part of you two. Save her the pain of knowing. Lord knows she's known enough. Don't do it again."

Frankie looked over at her with a raised eyebrow.

"I know, like I should talk. But why don't you be good for all the bad that I've been?"

"Can I still go back? Will she let me?"

"When she finally lets herself love you, she doesn't stop. If you want her, go get her. And make her happy. Maybe you can be all the things I never could. She deserves that."

"Is she home?"

"Follow the kite, and you'll find the woman," Romaine said, studying Frankie's face and thinking that Frankie would know Cleo in ways that she couldn't. Romaine winced a little, knowing it was finally over. She and Cleo would never be lovers again. It was a hard thing to know.

Frankie raced across town, pulling up in the drive and sending gravel flying. She watched Cleo maneuver the kite. She took a moment to look at the woman she would spend the rest of her life with, letting the thought penetrate her heart like the first ray of sun as it spreads across the landscape. She walked toward Cleo. Slowly a smile crept across Cleo's face. She knew why Frankie had come.

Frankie didn't say a word. She walked straight up to her, put her arms around Cleo, and kissed her deeply, trying to say with her body all the things she felt. Cleo kissed her back, letting the kite go, wrapping her body around Frankie.

Frankie looked into her eyes and said, "I love you, I want you, I need you. I don't care what's happened, I just want to be with you."

"Please," Cleo said, starting to cry.

Frankie wiped her tears away, kissing her, their tongues saying things words can't express.

Finally Cleo said, "Take me to bed before I seduce you right here in the middle of this dirt field."

"I'll make love with you anywhere," Frankie said, kissing her toward the back door.

Across town Romaine watched the kite bob and dive and finally crash to the ground, and she knew they'd found each other. She tried to be glad. She tried to hide the pang in her heart. It was letting go.

They slowly took each other's clothes off, each trying to memorize what the first time would be like, the first touch, the first time she gazes upon her lover's body, the first time she feels soft skin against soft skin.

Cleo gently pushed Frankie back on the bed and started to spread her legs.

"Wait a minute. I thought I was the top," Frankie chided.

"Do you know how often I've thought of this? How long I've wanted to do this?" Cleo said softly.

"And I haven't," Frankie said, pulling Cleo to her.

Cleo kissed her and pushed her on the bed more

insistently. "You'll just have to wait your turn," she said, kissing the insides of Frankie's thighs.

"I could be persuaded," Frankie said, feeling desire quicken her breathing and a low moan take hold as Cleo took her in her mouth.

Frankie ran her hand through Cleo's hair and pulled her close. She felt her breathing quicken and knew this was where she wanted and needed to be, in the arms of the woman who would love her until the end. Frankie cried out and pulled Cleo to her, feeling the weight of her slim body on top of her.

"I want to feel you," Frankie said, reaching inside Cleo's wet thighs.

They wrapped their bodies around one another and played deep into the night until there seemed to be no end to loving. Each time one awakened to see the other lying there, she would scoop the other up in her arms and whisper "I love you" until sleep came again.

Twenty-three

The light seemed odd in the room when Frankie awoke. She looked around for Cleo, but heard only noises from downstairs in the kitchen. She got up and found a T-shirt. Softly, she padded downstairs to the kitchen, praying nothing had changed from last night.

Cleo looked up at her and smiled. Frankie walked into her willing arms.

"God, I thought I'd done you in," Cleo said, brushing Frankie's hair back from her face. "I kept going upstairs to see if you were still breathing."

"How long have you been up?"

"All day."

"What time is it?"

"Dinnertime. Aren't you famished?"

"Dinnertime?" Frankie said, looking at the clock. "I slept all day?"

"Yes, darling. I hope this isn't a habit of yours."

"No, I haven't been sleeping much lately," Frankie replied, feeling a stab of guilt, thinking of her San Francisco liaison.

"I love you," Cleo said, holding her tight. "I thought about you all day. I couldn't quite believe that you were upstairs in my bed."

"Are you glad?"

"Very glad."

"Me too."

"Do you want to take a bath while I finish up?" Cleo asked.

"Why? Do I stink?"

"You smell well loved," Cleo said, pushing her away gently.

"Take one with me," Frankie said, pulling her in close again.

"I've got to watch dinner. It's our first romantic dinner together. Go look at the living room."

Frankie went to see. The low table with cushions had been set with a white linen tablecloth and a silver candelabra with eight candles.

"What were all the other dinners we had together?" Frankie asked, turning back around to Cleo.

"Those were preludes, promises of what might be. This is the real thing."

"I like this way better," Frankie said, kissing her.

Love is a strange thing, Frankie thought as she eased herself down into the steaming tub of water. *One moment I'm in torment, the next in ecstasy.* It's no wonder people can't stop falling in love. A morphine of the soul.

Cleo came in and washed her back.

"Better?" Frankie asked.

"Yes," Cleo said, taking her hand and holding it against Frankie's chest.

Frankie closed her eyes and wondered how she could ever have thought she could let this wonderful woman go.

They sat down to dinner. Frankie poured the wine and watched it sparkle in the candlelight.

Cleo caught her eye. "It looks beautiful."

"Not as beautiful as you."

"I love you," Cleo said, taking Frankie's face in her hands.

"You're a romantic at heart."

"As you will come to find out."

"Promise?"

"I promise. Romance for the rest of your days. If you want."

"I want," Frankie said, kissing her. "The only thing I'm really hungry for right now is you."

"Are you implying the food's not good?" Cleo chided, as Frankie moved closer, pushing back, kissing her neck.

"No, not at all, only you're better," Frankie said. She pulled Cleo's shirt off and took a breast in her mouth, then kissed her stomach before pulling her shorts off.

"I love your body," Frankie said, running her hands across Cleo's taut stomach. She lifted Cleo's hips higher, diving deep inside her with her mouth, watching Cleo close her eyes and melt with the moment. They finished dinner later, feeding each other, kissing in between.

Afterward, when they lay glistening together in the candlelight, Cleo asked, "Did you enjoy your first romantic dinner?"

"Very much," Frankie murmured.

They spent a whole week doing this.

"People are going to talk," Frankie said.

"Let them," Cleo said, wrapping her arms around Frankie as they lay on a blanket in the backyard, watching the clouds go by and guessing at their shapes.

They heard footsteps crunching on the rock path. It was Alice.

She smiled at them. "The community at large has asked that I come check on you two to see if you've fucked each other to death. It has been a week since anyone has seen you. Is this a vacation or a honeymoon?"

Frankie leaned up on one elbow. "I don't know. She hasn't asked."

"You haven't asked either," Cleo said, sitting up.

"It would be nice if you two would come around occasionally," Alice said.

"We will soon," Cleo responded, taking Frankie's hand and kissing it. She was just about to fall into Frankie's eyes when Alice stopped her.

"Whoa, before you two get going again, why don't

you come have a beer? It'll do you good to get some air. I'm not taking no for an answer. So get your butts up and come with," Alice said, tugging on Cleo's hand.

"All right already, one beer," Cleo said.

"It won't break the spell, I promise. You'll still be in love when you get back," Alice assured them.

Under duress they followed. Cleo recognized cars in the parking lot and glared at Alice.

"You didn't say the community at large would also be attending," Cleo said.

"Must have slipped my mind. They won't hurt you."

Cleo took Frankie's hand.

"Oh my god, the lovers make an appearance," Romaine said.

"We were about to send out a search party," Ella said.

"I'm sorry, Ella. I should have called," Frankie said, giving her a hug.

"I'm just glad things worked out," Ella said, smiling and patting Frankie on the back.

"Bobbi," Cleo said, hugging her.

"It appears she's forgiven us," Romaine said.

"I had to come see the woman who finally got your heart," Bobbi said, taking Frankie's hand.

"It's nice to meet you," Frankie said.

Alice got them drinks and they settled back to visit. But Frankie's thoughts kept straying. She found herself staring at Cleo and seeing her naked, responding to her touch. She saw her face as she closed her eyes in pleasure. She kept marveling at how she could touch her now, how tonight she would hold Cleo in her arms, beneath covers, smooth skin touching. Cleo reached out and took her hand beneath the table. Frankie's long, cool fingers closed in on her own.

Bobbi watched them and caught Romaine's eye, knowing they both felt a pang for it. Frankie had the one woman they'd both loved.

Romaine got up and poured herself another drink. Bobbi followed.

"This hurts, doesn't it," Bobbi said quietly.

Romaine looked at her, feeling the flood of damage she had imposed.

"Yes, it hurts. Hurts like hell. When are you going to find some incredible woman to bring around and remind me of what fool I was?" Romaine said ruefully.

"I tried, remember. She wouldn't have me. She only wanted you."

"Yeah, and I botched it," Romaine said, making a martini.

"Make me one of those, will you?" Bobbi said.

"This isn't easy for you either," Romaine said, looking at her softly.

"No, I loved you both and lost you both. I won't recover any time soon," Bobbi said.

"Another casualty in this war of hearts. Perhaps now that it's done, you'll be the last one. Not that that makes it any easier for you," Romaine said, looking across the bar at Cynthia.

"No, it doesn't," Bobbi said, taking her drink and joining the others. She'd never forgive Romaine for coming into her life, for making her love her, for leaving, for letting Cleo get close and then walking away. She loved both of them, and somehow she couldn't get either one of them out of her system.

Romaine finally got disgusted and dismissed Frankie and Cleo.

"You two go home, fuck some more until you're thoroughly sick of each other, and then come back around. Right now you're hopeless," Romaine said, pushing them to the door. Gladly, they left, kissing frantically the moment they were alone as if it had been too long already.

Romaine and Cynthia left shortly after.

"I know this is hard for you," Cynthia said, squeezing Romaine's hand.

Romaine nodded and let her into the car. She tried to compose herself before she got in. Romaine didn't want Cynthia to see her hurting.

"You know what's the worst part, the hardest part to take, is the way Cleo looks at her, the look of total love. She used to look at me that way until I started hurting her," Romaine said, swallowing hard.

"Someone looks at you that way now," Cynthia said, turning Romaine's head. "I do."

Romaine scooped Cynthia up in her arms. She kissed her face, her eyes, her mouth.

Alice poured Ella another drink. "So you think it'll work?"

"This swapping partners stuff? I hope so. I think

Cleo and Romaine have gone too far to come back now. They've got to cut the cord or kill themselves trying," Ella said.

"It's the ones in between I worry about. I don't want Cynthia and Frankie to be like the others," Alice said, knitting her brow and silently praying Cupid was right for once. He seemed notorious for misdirections.

Frankie grabbed Cleo the moment they walked in the door.

"You've been away much too long," Frankie said, nuzzling Cleo's neck and steadily working her way down until she found a breast to suckle. Then Frankie reached lower.

"I was right next to you the whole time," Cleo said, as Frankie happily found her wet and willing.

"Yes, close but not close enough," Frankie said, closing her eyes and flattening Cleo against the closet door.

Cleo thought her knees would give out, yet she pulled Frankie closer and dipped her hand into loosened jeans, her fingers going quickly inside, making Frankie cry out.

"I don't think I've ever made love there," Cleo said, holding Frankie tight, her body slowly relaxing.

"Now will you take a bath with me?" Frankie said smiling.

"I'd love to," Cleo said, taking her hand and leading her upstairs.

* * * * *

Frankie was lying on Cleo's stomach in the hot soapy bath.

"I was thinking..." Cleo said.

"Yes," Frankie said, snuggling up close.

"You know, when Ella asked you about coming home."

"I probably should make an appearance soon. I have been borrowing clothes for a week now."

"I know, but I want you to make this your home," Cleo said, looking serious. She'd thought about it last night as she listened to Frankie's even breathing, as she gazed on her face. She needed to jump, plunge into all she was afraid of. Strange, she almost understood Romaine for half a second, her holding women at arm's length, afraid of getting close because their experience of closeness had always threatened to suffocate them both. Living with your lover was the only real way to get close. But could you get that and not suffocate? Cleo was willing to try.

"Sounds like an awfully big step," Frankie said.

"But look at all the trouble taking small steps created. I don't want to date. I want us to be together, like a couple."

"Like married?" Frankie said, raising an inquisitive eyebrow.

"No. Romaine and I were married, and look where that got us. More like commitment," Cleo said.

"You mean I don't get to be your wife? You wound me to the core," Frankie said, putting her hand over her heart.

"I want you to be my partner, my best friend, my lover."

"Is that better than being a wife?"

"Much."

"All right then, I'll think about it," Frankie said.

Cleo's face went serious. "You'll think about it?"

"There is all my furniture to consider," Frankie replied.

"Furniture, what furniture? If you don't want to live here, we could find somewhere else."

"Cleo, I love this house. I love you. I'm messing around, diffusing the seriousness. I'm scared. But it doesn't mean I don't want to try. I want to, I do."

Cleo cupped her hands softly around Frankie's buttocks and drew her near.

"I was hoping you would."

Later in the dark, Frankie said, "Cleo?"

"Yes."

"I really do want to live with you. I can't imagine dating. It just doesn't seem like something we could do. I'm either with you or not, but I couldn't stand to be halfway."

Cleo pulled her close. "Neither could I."

"Can you stand me as a roommate?"

"Well, you appear to be relatively neat, and you love my cooking. Those are my two most important requirements."

"Would you still love me if I wasn't neat?"

"It would be difficult, but I'd try. Why? Have you been faking neatness all this time?"

"No, ma'am."

"Are you scared?"

"Yes."

"Me too. But we'll talk about things. Okay?"

"Will you come with me on the road sometimes?"

"Are you afraid to leave me in town?"

"No. I trust you, and I think I understand what happened. I want the sensation of having you there with me, watching. I want to come offstage and have the woman I love standing there. I know it's weird, but when I'm done, I feel so vulnerable. I want you to hold me and make me strong again. Is that odd?"

"No, it's beautiful. You're beautiful."

"Show me," Frankie said, sliding her hand in between Cleo's legs.

Twenty-four

Frankie stood on the deck and watched the sunset. Thinking back to her sojourn on the beach, to having Sunday dinners with her wife's ex-wife, she laughed. She had never thought this would happen. Life always produced those strange turnarounds just when you thought impossibility lay etched in some primordial stone. Like a stick caught in a river, fluidity grabbed you and off you went, riding the crest of the obstacle. Change proved nothing was truly stable, nothing fixed enough to ever achieve permanence. *Hang around in your life long enough and it too will change.*

They were having dinner at Romaine and Cynthia's new house. Romaine finally got the house in the hills that she always wanted. As they had driven up there, Frankie had asked Cleo if she wanted a house in the hills.

Cleo had put her hand on Frankie's knee. "No, darling. I like it simple."

"Is that why you like me? 'Cause I'm simple?"

"You're far from simple. You're my complex musician with an eye for the sardonic. I wouldn't call that simple. I listen to the words. I know better than to think what's on the surface is all that's there."

"Are you sure this is what you want?"

"What are trying to do, tell me it's over?" Cleo said, looking slightly alarmed.

Frankie looked down at her hands. "No. I love you more than ever. I'm just nervous about this dinner thing."

"Why didn't you say so? We didn't have to go."

"I know. Romaine makes me nervous. She intimidates me."

Cleo took her hand as they rounded the bend. "You're twice the woman she'll ever be, and I've never been this happy."

"I know. It's just that you two have so much past. I feel like a newcomer, and I don't know where I fit in."

Cleo pulled the car over to the side of the road.

"Get out."

"Are you throwing me out?"

"No, I want to do something. Come on."

They stood on the side of the mountain.

"You don't suffer from vertigo, do you?"

"Sometimes," Frankie said, looking down at the sharp, stone-studded incline.

"Don't look down. Raise your right hand," Cleo instructed.

Frankie obeyed. "What are we doing?"

"It's called the promise prayer."

"Is this something you and Romaine did?"

"No, this is something you and I are doing."

"What is its origin then?"

"I made it up."

"When?"

"Just now," Cleo said.

"Why are we doing this?"

"Because it's time. Now repeat after me: I promise before the goddess and woman to love, honor, and cherish you, and never sleep with another woman in our bed until the end of our days, not because we have to but because we want to."

Frankie repeated it.

"Does this mean we're married?" Frankie asked.

"Yes," Cleo responded. "Aren't you going to kiss the bride?"

"Who's the bride?"

"I am. You're the top, remember?"

Frankie kissed her.

"I thought you didn't want to get married?" Frankie chided.

"It's a woman's prerogative to change her mind."

"Did you and Romaine get married?"

"It's in bad taste to mention previous lovers at one's wedding."

"But did you?"

"No. So see, she's not really my ex-wife."

"I love you," Frankie said, "and I'm glad you're my wife."

"Me too. Feel better?"

"Yes. After all, it is my wedding day," Frankie said, smiling.

"Exactly. Now let's go eat, and then we'll start the honeymoon."

"I can hardly wait," Frankie said, scooping Cleo up in her arms.

A slow smile crept across Frankie's face as she reenacted the scene of her wedding day, something she knew she'd do for years to come.

"You look like the cat that swallowed the canary," Romaine said.

Frankie turned abruptly. She thought she was alone. She met Romaine's gaze.

"Nice house," Frankie said.

"You like it? I've wanted this place for a long time. It just never worked out before," Romaine said, leaning on the railing.

Romaine had left Cleo helping Cynthia make the salad. They were chatting amiably when she left them, and it had made her feel strange, something like jealousy, remorse, love, and loss all in the same muddled moment. She left feeling confused, like something wasn't quite right.

Wife and mistress in the same room, in a house she had dreamed of, filled with both of the women she had wanted. But only one lived here. Sometimes it felt like it wasn't the right one. And she knew it might hurt forever. It seemed that Cleo was done with hurting. She was glowing with a happiness Romaine hadn't seen before and was no longer a part of.

The thought of Cleo living with someone else was still a fresh wound. She kept remembering Cleo's telling her that Frankie was living with her. They were at the café. Romaine had tried to quickly hide the hurt in her eyes. She knew it was inevitable, but she couldn't keep from feeling sad. Cleo caught it and wrapped her arms around her, whispering, "It'll be okay." But it wasn't and it wouldn't be for a long time.

"Are you happy?" Romaine said, meeting Frankie's eyes.

"Yes. Are you?"

"Yes and no, but then it's always been like that. Nothing new," Romaine said, looking out across the landscape.

"Why aren't you happy? You've got this beautiful house and a wife who loves you more than you deserve."

"You're right."

"You still miss her don't you?"

"I'll always miss her. I can't make myself stop. You've made her so happy, something I never could do. I feel like such a shit. I give Cynthia what I can. It's not the same. It's not what it should be. I just can't make myself let go. Letting Cleo go is like losing the only part of myself I really ever knew."

"Why are you telling me this?"

"Because you're the only one I can tell."

"Are you asking me to give her back?" Frankie said, feeling her fingers furl the railing.

"No, that wouldn't work, for any of us. The one thing I've discovered out of this mess is that at some point we stop being kind, stop trying to make the one we love happy, and it's then the cruelty begins. The cruelty becomes a habit, an addictive, incurable habit. Something to remember, because once it starts there's no going back. Even if I could get Cleo back, I couldn't stop being cruel. She's safer with you. Maybe the two of you will never start being mean to each other."

"Are you cruel to Cynthia?"

"I have been. I try to watch myself. But like any addict, I'll fall. We enjoy good times knowing they will come crashing down when I go off bingeing again."

"Would you go back to Cleo if you could?"

"Do you want my honest answer or the answer that I'm supposed to give for the welfare of everyone?"

"I want your honest answer."

"I would go back if she'd let me," Romaine said, looking directly at Frankie. Their eyes met.

"What about Cynthia?"

"She would hate me like all the others."

"If you could go back, would you be true to Cleo and love her honestly for the rest of your days?"

"I'd like to think I've learned from this, but I don't know if I could trust myself enough to say that," Romaine said, studying her hands.

"Then you can't have her," Frankie said.

"You'd give her to me?" Romaine asked, puzzled, wondering if there was trouble in paradise.

"She's not mine to give, but I would let her go if I thought you would be true."

"Why?"

"Because I love her."

"So you'd let her go? I'm confused."

"I love her, but I'm not the love of her life. You are. There will always be a ghost between us, and no matter how hard we try you'll always be there."

"I'm sorry," Romaine said, feeling a rush of remorse. "I've really fucked with the cosmic laws of love."

"You have," Frankie said, looking out at the view and feeling sadder than she ever had.

Romaine studied her for a moment.

"With time, those scars will heal, and you'll make her happier than I ever could. Believe it or not, you are everything Cleo always wanted me to be. I'll never be those things. We were together for a long time, and when you two have spent that much time together there will be no more ghosts. I'll be no more than a friend, and all the memories that plague you now will be nothing; all the memories will be of the two of you. Frankie, don't give up. She loves you, and she needs you. Please."

"Are you giving her to me?"

"She's not mine to give, but she's yours if you'll let her be," Romaine said.

Frankie smiled. "You mean that?"

"I do."

Frankie extended her hand. "Friends?"

"Of course," Romaine said, taking her hand and shaking it. Then she put her arm across Frankie's shoulders.

"Did you ever think we'd be standing here like this?"

"Never," Frankie said. "Did you?"

"No," Romaine said.

Cleo looked out the picture window at the two women she loved and smiled. It was getting better, and someday it would be wonderful. *Life is the queerest thing,* she thought, shaking her head.

Cynthia called from the kitchen. "Where are those two?"

"I think they're making amends."

"And what about us?" Cynthia said, coming to her side.

"We were never enemies; we were victims."

"What are we now?" Cynthia asked.

"Victors with bodacious spoils," Cleo replied.

"Funny how we always use battle metaphors for love," Cynthia said.

"Darling, love is nothing but an endless revolution."

"It's time to feed the troops."

"Shall I blow the bugle?"

"Please."

A few of the publications of
THE NAIAD PRESS, INC.
P.O. Box 10543 • Tallahassee, Florida 32302
Phone (904) 539-5965
Toll-Free Order Number: 1-800-533-1973
*Mail orders welcome. Please include 15% postage.
Write or call for our free catalog which also features an incredible selection of lesbian videos.*

HOT CHECK by Peggy J. Herring. 192 pp. Will workaholic Alice fall for guitarist Ricky? ISBN 1-56280-163-5 $11.95

OLD TIES by Saxon Bennett. 176 pp. Can Cleo surrender to a passionate new love? ISBN 1-56280-159-7 11.95

LOVE ON THE LINE by Laura DeHart Young. 176 pp. Will Stef win Kay's heart? ISBN 1-56280-162-7 $11.95

DEVIL'S LEG CROSSING by Kaye Davis. 192 pp. 1st Maris Middleton mystery. ISBN 1-56280-158-9 11.95

COSTA BRAVA by Marta Balletbo Coll. 144 pp. Read the book, see the movie! ISBN 1-56280-153-8 11.95

MEETING MAGDALENE & OTHER STORIES by Marilyn Freeman. 144 pp. Read the book, see the movie! ISBN 1-56280-170-8 11.95

SECOND FIDDLE by Kate Calloway. 208 pp. P.I. Cassidy James' second case. ISBN 1-56280-169-6 11.95

LAUREL by Isabel Miller. 128 pp. By the author of the beloved *Patience and Sarah.* ISBN 1-56280-146-5 10.95

LOVE OR MONEY by Jackie Calhoun. 240 pp. The romance of real life. ISBN 1-56280-147-3 10.95

SMOKE AND MIRRORS by Pat Welch. 224 pp. 5th Helen Black Mystery. ISBN 1-56280-143-0 10.95

DANCING IN THE DARK edited by Barbara Grier & Christine Cassidy. 272 pp. Erotic love stories by Naiad Press authors. ISBN 1-56280-144-9 14.95

These are just a few of the many Naiad Press titles — we are the oldest and largest lesbian/feminist publishing company in the world. We also offer an enormous selection of lesbian video products. Please request a complete catalog. We offer personal service; we encourage and welcome direct mail orders from individuals who have limited access to bookstores carrying our publications.